Avery & Aria

The Story of Star-Crossed Lovers

Avery & Aria

The Story of Star-Crossed Lovers

Avery & Aria

© Copyright 2021 Viola Tempest

Cover Design by Marginean Anca Gabriela at BRoseDesignz

Table of Contents

Chapter One
Avery's Story
Reminiscing the Past
14

Chapter Two
Avery's Story
Childhood Crush
27

Chapter Three
Aria's Story
My First Kiss
39

Chapter Four
Avery's Story
My First Rejection
53

Table of Contents

Chapter Five
Aria's Story
Conflicted Feelings
68

Chapter Six
Aria's Story
Truth or Dare
80

Chapter Seven
Jessica's Story
My Boyfriend Avery
93

Chapter Eight
Aria's Story
Too Little, Too Late
104

Table of Contents

Chapter Nine
Avery's Story
Karma
112

Chapter Ten
Aria's Story
Addicted to Love
120

Chapter Eleven
Avery's Story
Just a One-Night Stand, Right?
135

Chapter Twelve
Aria's Story
Friends Reconnected
142

Table of Contents

Chapter Thirteen
Avery's Story
Feelings Returned
150

Chapter Fourteen
Liana's Story
No More Mr. Nice Guy
163

Chapter Fifteen
Aria's Story
Best Friends Forever
170

Chapter Sixteen
Avery's Story
The Unexpected Betrayal
183

Table of Contents

Chapter Seventeen
Aria's Story
All Alone Once Again
199

Avery & Aria

Chapter One

Avery's Story
Reminiscing the Past

Hi, my name is Avery Cheung.

I always considered myself to be a normal, average guy, as normal as normal could be, anyway. By the time I was in my mid-20s, I was already dominating the world of Wall Street. I'd done very well for myself, professionally, over the previous decade, earning myself the title of one of the country's youngest entrepreneurs.

I graduated top of my class with degrees in both finance and economics at one of the most prestigious universities in the country, and by the time I entered my late 20s, I was making close to a million dollars a year. I had a beautiful wife and two lovely children, all of whom respected me, and I lived in the upscale part of Manhattan in New York City.

I literally couldn't ask for anything more.

So why did I still feel so lonely, so miserable? As if, none of those things even mattered?

I stared out the window of my 31st floor office, letting out a loud sigh and taking the fifth sip of my whiskey. Just another miserable day working a miserable job I no longer found any passion in.

Don't get me wrong, the view from the Walden building was phenomenal, an architectural masterpiece that magically blended the man-made wonder with the beauty of the metropolitan city. However, despite all the wonders and beauty around me, I felt nothing but dread in my life. Like there was a piece of me missing, something I knew could make me feel complete...

If only I had it, if only I had her.

Not even my cleaned-pressed suit and freshly-polished shoes could lift my spirits from the dark cloud I'd been living under, battling constantly with myself to save face in front of my family while also feeling like I had nothing left to lose. Every day at work, I received the highest compliments anyone could receive, and yet, none of it mattered. Maybe it's just my reputation keeping me respected and honored because, in reality, I knew I had been a mess, showing up late, skipping meetings, and mouthing off to my shareholders.

But it's not all for nothing. I had my reasons. Two weeks prior, I received a rather surprising text from Aria Xing, a young woman with little presence but many memories in my life, a woman I had never forgotten. I'd known Aria since we were just two young innocent souls who had just happened to get enrolled in the same preschool, but our connection quickly blossomed into a beautiful friendship soon after.

Ah, I remembered the days. We used to be inseparable… But that was a long time ago, drifting apart and reuniting only to drift apart once again. We never really did get the timing right, always chasing after each other only when the other stopped caring or became unavailable.

I used to think Aria was the one, the one I was destined to be with ever since we were kids, but every time I confessed my love to her, it never seemed to be reciprocated. Don't get me wrong, I did try fighting for her, many times, constantly giving her chances and the willingness to drop everything and everyone else for her.

That Aria, never really could make up her mind on what she wanted. Eventually, I stopped hearing from her after several years and thought that was the end of that.

Only a short while after I thought Aria and I had separated for good, I met my wife, Liana May. I met Liana during a dark time in my life, a time I wanted to forget but also remember as an important milestone. She provided me with some much-needed services and was there for me when I needed comforting arms until I finally asked her out on a real date.

I knew I wanted to marry her when we went walking by the pier one early morning, carrying around our lattes we had just gotten from a new café in town. I remembered her slipping on a kid's skateboard and bumping into me, which caused us both to fall over and spill our drinks on a man sitting on a nearby bench.

Boy, was he mad. No one should have to start their day with two hot and fresh cups of lattes decorating their suit, but all Liana and I could do was laugh. That's when I knew I wanted to marry her. She was just so easy-going and low maintenance, a partner who was always there for me without all the drama and insecurity.

I had the perfect woman, the perfect wife who treated me like a king and was willing to sacrifice her whole life so I could achieve mine, giving up her dream job as a paralegal to care for the kids so I could continue chasing mine.

I loved Liana with all my heart, so why was I standing here thinking about Aria?

It had been years since I last spoke to Aria. After failing to hear from her for half a decade, I decided to finally give up on that dream and move on. Liana had been nothing but compassionate and pleasant in my life, much different from Aria. To be honest, after three long years of marriage, I had almost pushed Aria out of my mind completely…until the night she texted me.

Aria: Hey, Avery. I miss you. Grab a drink with me soon?

I didn't text her back, for obvious reasons, but during those past two weeks, Aria had been all I could think about. Of course, Liana had no idea; I could never break her heart like that, not again. Hell, we almost didn't get married because I had been so fixated on my past that I almost left my wife at the altar and walked away.

But truth was, even though I'd moved on, I never stopped thinking about Aria, not even for a second.

Aria, Aria, why now? Why text me back now when I'm supposed to be happily married?

But no matter how hard I tried, I couldn't stop thinking about all the *what ifs* I could have with Aria as my limbs tickled with the sudden urge to leave, to just leave everything I'd worked so hard for behind and rush back to the love of my life. She's like a drug, an addiction that brings with her quick pleasure and everlasting consequences. And I was allowing it to all consume me.

Nothing, even my vows and my children, could ever triumph the connection and bond I felt towards Aria Xing.

Sometimes I swore I could hear Aria's sweet voice whispering in my ear, calling my name in a low and distinct voice. It reminded me of when we used to be the best of friends. When we used to be more than that. I'd hear her, and I'd feel her touching my skin in a way only she could…

No, I couldn't think like that. I couldn't even think about thinking like that. All she had ever given me, from the day I met her, was pain, confusion, and misery. She ruined me, ruined my life and everything I thought I could have. I trusted her, cared for her even when she treated me like shit, just for her to turn around and leave me once again, always apologizing for running away and acting like nothing ever happened.

But I couldn't blame her completely. If I hadn't forgiven her all these years, she wouldn't have gotten the chance to hurt me again…and again…and again.

My thoughts were suddenly interrupted by a knock on my office door that stopped my emotional rollercoaster ride. I gently closed my eyes and faced the wall, letting out a sigh of annoyance and disappointment.

The vivacity I used to have when I was younger had been torn down by the waves of flashbacks overwhelming my mind. I used to be so focused, so diligent, but my mind was now wandering and wondering about what could've been.

I was stuck in the past, the past of regret, and most of the time, I didn't even know how to get out.

"Mr. Cheung, your wife is on the other line," my secretary, Kimiko Sakamoto, said as she walked into my office.

I opened my eyes, the notion of losing someone I loved hitting me all over again.

"Tell her I'm busy with a project. And don't disturb me again until I tell you so," I confided with a heavy voice.

"Yes, sir," Kimiko answered promptly, closing the door quietly as she departed.

I was already known as the stern stick-in-the-mud at work, even before I saw that text from Aria. Now, I had become a real jackass.

Memories from the past captured me again, and the desire to see Aria compelled me into searching through a secret folder in my phone to find one of her old pictures. I kept every picture I had ever taken of or with Aria, struggling to find the strength to delete them. I was not known to be a sentimental guy, barely having more than five photos of my family in total, and even those were only the ones professionally taken from major events.

But with Aria, I couldn't even count how many I had of her.

And with the power of password protection, Liana would never find out. It was my little secret. I stared nostalgically at the first one, from the day we first met, and I let the memories take me.

Melancholy always retained me, like an entity forcing me to still live in the past. I swiped to another picture, one where I was sitting alone with Aria, age 9. This was taken just seconds after I had scraped my knee, and Aria was devoted to dressing my wound. I always told her she'd make a great nurse, but she always cringed at the thought of cleaning up sick patients.

I scoffed as I looked at her adorable smile, concern in her eyes. "You were such a sweetheart," I smiled as I caressed the picture on the screen. "What happened to you?"

She looked just as I remembered her to be in that picture. A beautiful girl with midnight black hair braided in an intricate pigtail, and a huge grin adorning her cute face. She owned the world back then; she owned it all. Even me.

***

I still remembered the first day of preschool as if it had happened yesterday. It was the day we first met. I was about five years old, and I knew that I had a pretty distinctive look and a sharp mind, both of which deterred most people, but not Aria. That's when I first knew that she was special, like me.

My family and I had just arrived to the states from far away mainland China, and at first, no one wanted to be around me. They all saw me as different, as someone who didn't belong in their world, a foreigner. No one wanted to talk to me. I felt like such an outcast.

All I wanted to do when I first stepped foot into America was make friends and be around people. Growing up in China and having only my family around me, I felt so alone. Sure, my parents were always around me, taking care of me and giving me what I needed, but there were never any kids my age around to hang out with. I lived in an isolated village that no one ever visited because it was so remote that it was almost unreachable.

When I said goodbye to my mom and stepped foot inside that classroom the first day, kids were weeping all around me, with several others as confused as I was. At that moment, I felt so scared, and I almost cried for my mom.

But I knew I couldn't. I knew I had to be brave for her. My parents gave up everything, their entire lives in China, just to give me a better one in the states. The least I could do was survive preschool. Feeling out of place, I pulled my juice box out from my backpack and sat down alone on an empty chair, refusing to make eye contact with anyone. Then I heard a sweet voice.

"Hi! I'm Aria. Is this your first day?" the voice said cheerfully.

Slowly looking up, I saw her, the most adorable girl I had ever seen in the five years of my existence. It was obvious, even at first glance, that she was different. She was calm, regardless of the mayhem around her. She looked older than the rest of us, like she knew something we didn't. And I liked it.

With a meek voice, I whispered, "yes," and nodded.

Then she sat down next to me, like she knew exactly how I was feeling, the empathy I had always been so envious of.

"You miss your mom, don't you?" she asked, placing a hand on my shoulder.

I didn't know what I was feeling, but her hand sent a tingling sensation throughout my body, and I nodded.

"It's okay," she continued. "I miss my mom too, and my dad, but it's only for a couple hours. Before you know it, she'll be back to pick you up! You'll like it here, trust me. This is a great school. We have nap time and snack time and… Hey! Do you want one of my egg tarts? My dad gave me one too many this morning, and there's no way I can finish both of them."

As Aria handed me one of her egg tarts and smiled, I gracefully accepted it and smiled back.

"Thanks," I whispered. "I love egg tarts. They're my favorite."

"Don't worry about it! They're my favorite too! I think you'll like it here once you get to know some people. I was shy at first, but now, I love coming here. Don't worry, I'll be your friend," Aria eagerly cheered as she sat down next to me.

She was wearing a pink jacket with matching shoes and bows in her pigtails. Her eyes looked similar to mine, but a bit larger and hazel brown, sparkling a hint of innocence.

Over the next several minutes, we both sat there in silence, nibbling on our tarts. She was so optimistic, so open-minded. I knew right then and there that I wanted to be her friend. As we ate, we stared off into the crowd. Even in preschool, cliques were already being formed, and it was clear that I wasn't going to be part of one.

As I sat there, lost in my thoughts about my life back in China and whether I belonged here, I felt a nudge against my arm.

"What's your name?" she asked me.

I looked over and whispered, "Avery. Avery Cheung."

She smiled at me when the teacher walked in, interrupting our conversation. Mrs. Leung. None of the kids in that classroom liked her. She always came into the classroom bitter and angry, like she woke up on the wrong side of bed.

We spent the rest of the day together, and I thought it was fate, written in the fortunes of our lives. I was a shy kid, and Aria had mesmerized me with her stunning giggles and fascinating chatter. Even when I didn't feel like talking, she brought me out of my shell, and I felt like I belonged. She refused to leave me alone, and even though I sometimes found that annoying, I was glad she didn't.

When my mother picked me up later that day, she gave me a long hug and asked me how my day was. "Did you make any friends?"

Looking behind me, I tried to find Aria, but she was nowhere in sight. I turned back to my mother, "Sort of. I think."

She could only chuckle at my response. "Come on, we need to go home and get ready. We're having dinner at one of our neighbors tonight. Your dad and I met them while grocery shopping and found out that they're from the same part of China as we are. Such a wonderful coincidence! They have a daughter about your age. Maybe you two will get along and become the best of friends."

Mom smiled at me, excited about the chance for me to make new friends, but all I could feel were butterflies in my stomach. If it wasn't for Aria, I would never have made friends that first day. Oh geez. What was I going to do? I'd always been a socially-awkward kid; that was never going to change.

Maybe I can just sit there in silence for three hours and hope no one calls me out.

"I think we'll get along very well with the Xing's," Mom spoke cheerfully as she drove us home.

When I walked through the front door, dragging my backpack behind me, my dad had a wide smile on his face and a mini bow tie and blazer in his hands. I knew that was my suit for the night as I grabbed them both and slowly trudged upstairs.

Why did I have to go anyway? It's just going to be a bunch of old adults sitting around and talking about their boring jobs while I stand awkwardly around kids I don't even know. I'd much rather hang out with Aria. At least she gets me.

An hour later, we arrived at the Xing's. They didn't live too far away from us, just a couple streets away. My dad rang the doorbell, and a boy, slightly older than me, opened the door.

"Mom!" he yelled out before putting his headphones over his ears and running up the stairs, away from the strangers.

Geez, the manners on that kid, I thought. I had hoped that he wasn't the kid I was supposed to hang out with. I would hate to be friends with someone who didn't even have enough manners to say hello to his guests.

"Hi! So good to see you both again. And I'm guessing this is little Avery," a woman smiled as she leaned in towards me. "I think you'll get along quite well with my Aria. Aria, sweetie! Come down, and say hi to our guests."

Aria? I thought. *Could it be? No, it couldn't be. It was too good to be true.*

As I remained lost in my thoughts, suddenly, a familiar face with pigtails and a pink dress came running down the stairs.

"Avery!" Aria screamed with joy as she raced towards me and hugged me.

Chapter Two

From that day on, Aria and I became inseparable, the best of friends. We went from being classmates to neighbors to best friends. Avery and Aria. Aria and Avery. I never knew how I got so lucky to meet someone as great as Aria. She was smart, compassionate, and even at that young age, I felt my heart and body gravitating toward her.

I didn't know what instigated it, but I knew that I wanted to be by Aria's side forever and protect her.

Aria's personality didn't differ too much from mine. When we first met, I thought she was an extrovert, always interacting with people and getting to know them.

But as the years went on, I started to realize that she was more like me, an introvert who kept to herself and saw the world for what it truly was rather than the rainbows and unicorns we had been taught. We were both equally weird introverts. Of course, we'd try to hide it from everyone else to avoid being isolated by our friends.

We were friends with Jesper Xi and Rosalie Zhao. I was never a fan of them, but they were Aria's closest friends so I had to pretend to play nice. It's not like they liked me much either. Without Aria, we would've never even thought about being friends.

Those two were definitely extroverts, full of liveliness and optimism about a life that would never come to fruition, while Aria and I remained pessimists who hated the world and wanted to watch it burn. I liked it that way, always keeping each other full of surprises.

Sigh, Aria, her smile always full of sparkles and shine that proved breathtaking. Though she was sometimes quiet around others, she was always an open book around me, always sharing with me her secrets, as embarrassing as they were, her eyes often speaking of untold truths.

Like I said, I was a very quiet child and didn't have much friends. Aria was the only person I was close to. She was genuine, unlike some of her friends we'd hang out with. Her beautiful hazel eyes were always mesmerizing, and her smile always shined in a notorious smirk. I knew back then, at a very young age, that I was blinded by love. Even as I got older, I found myself never really falling out of love with her.

She was…Aria.

***

Overwhelmed by the memories, I tried to look away, to close the images, but for some reason, I couldn't stop myself from scrolling through more and more pictures. I couldn't remember exactly when I fell for Aria, when I even began to like girls, but even though I always wanted more, she always just saw me as her friend, her best friend who would never do anything to betray or hurt her.

But what did I know? I was just a kid, too young and naïve to know what I was feeling.

After all, we *were* just kids, confusing love and affection with just wanting a friend and someone to hang out with. I knew I felt lonely on that first day. Maybe I was so desperate to belong, to feel wanted, that I mistook friendliness for love. I just wanted her to be by my side that day, to be able to indulge in her presence.

Or so that's what I thought it was. Decades later, I still had the same exact feelings.

I scrolled back to a picture of when we were just 8-years old, Aria caring for my bruised and scraped knee after I fell off my bike. I sat on my chair, leaned back, closed my eyes, and let my memory take over me, traveling back in time to when I was 8-years old. Aria and I were riding our bikes together back from school when she surprised me with a dare.

***

"Hey, Avery! Let's race! Last one home is a chicken!" Aria yelled out with a smirk.

Before I even had a chance to respond, she was off. It's in my nature to be competitive, much like it was also in Aria's nature. I hated to lose, so off I went after her, and boy, was she fast! As she zoomed past me, her body leaning forward against the handlebars and pedaling as fast as she could, I felt myself struggling to catch up, swerving in all directions.

A few minutes into the race, I lost my balance, a twig snagging my wheel, and seconds later, I found myself flying off my bike. As the bike collided with a tree, I slid across the concrete, tearing apart my knees and elbows. It didn't take long for Aria to notice what had happened as she no longer had someone screaming after her. She looked back, found me crying on the ground, and rushed over to help me.

"Avery! Are you okay? I'm so sorry!" she exclaimed as tears welled in her eyes. "Let me help you!"

As I grabbed onto her hand, I felt tingles shiver through my body, a sensation I had never felt from anyone else. I still remembered how she tore off the sleeve of her shirt and dressed my wound before helping me home, always so caring. She was such a kind friend, a beautiful girl, one I always admired and looked up to.

Mom always loved Aria, seeing her as her own daughter, and she'd praise Aria for taking care of me. Honestly, I couldn't ask for a better friend. She would treasure every moment Aria and I spent together, taking pictures of us with her polaroid camera, and always telling us that we would be best friends forever.

Even at a young age, Mom always told me that Aria was the one, the one I was destined to be with. Of course, I was too young to even think about that, but I didn't exactly disagree with her either.

***

I scrolled through a next set of pictures, my face blushing as I remembered each embarrassing moment. It was the day I realized Aria was paying more attention to me than I'd thought. They were pictures from one of my birthday parties.

The first picture showed my home, entirely decorated with blue and pink balloons, our favorite colors, and other birthday ornaments. The main door had multicolored ribbons, and there were multitudinous streamers and sparkling ornaments throughout the halls.

I remembered it well. In the kitchen, there was a huge table, 6 feet by 4 feet, wholly filled with gifts for me, although I had only one true friend. But everyone loved Aria, and they all showed up just to be around her.

It was also because all the parents in the neighborhood wanted to meet mine, the newcomers in a town that barely had new residents. I didn't know half the people there, and I'd much rather spend time alone with Aria than have to entertain people I didn't care about. It wasn't a surprise to me that most of the pictures showed me alone and uncomfortable in the crowds. That pretty much summed up my entire life.

I scrolled to another picture, a picture of me standing by the door, my eyes looking far into the distance, oblivious to the camera. I remembered waiting, waiting for one special person. Her. The party was a drag without her presence. I stood there, unmoving and unfazed by the party raging around me, until a beautiful girl walked in, her parents by her side, and a present in her hands.

And there she was, wearing a baby pink maxi dress. Her hair was loosely curled, and her bangs were perfectly cut, as always.

The picture of perfection.

***

"Hey, birthday boy! Ready for your punches?" she joked as she handed me the neatly wrapped box decorated with a beautiful blue bow. "I hope you like this. I wrapped it myself!"

"Thanks, short stack," I replied with a smirk.

"Hey, stop it!" Aria frowned. "You're not that much taller than me! You know I'm sensitive when it comes to my height," she complained.

We continued that argument for years, and I kept at it because I liked the way her lips pouted when she got annoyed at me.

"Okay, medium stack," I jokingly corrected myself. "By the way, what is this?" I gave the present a little shake.

"I don't know, open it," Aria frowned again, the frown soon turning into a smile.

Frowning was a thing she did so often, her perpetually sad face. I sometimes thought that expression was like her default reaction when she didn't know what to do with her face or what emotion to show, much like how I always grinned like a clown whenever I didn't know what emotion to show.

The rest of the party went well, but the whole time, I was waiting for the guests to leave so I could open my best friend's present. When the time finally came, I tore apart the wrapping paper nervously. I found another box inside, and when I opened it, I was surprised to find a sketchbook, some acrylic paints, a sketch pencil, and some other painting and sketching utensils.

On top of it all, there was a handwritten note. One I had snapped a picture of years later in case I ever lost the original.

Hey Avery,

It's your birthday. Happy birthday to you! I know you never told me about your secret hobby (and it shouldn't be a secret at all), but I somehow figured out that you like to draw, like... sketches... of me (Btw,

I love them, and I have seen them, but shhh, I won't tell anyone) or nature, or maybe other things too that I haven't found out about yet. Just draw whenever and whatever you like. If you wanna keep it a secret, that's okay with me.
Hope you like my gift.
Your best friend,
Aria

***

I smiled again as I read it, the same idiot smile I had on my face the first time I read it. It was right then and there that I actually felt like she saw me as more than just a friend. She noticed me, unlike many others who just saw me as a walking brain. Aria saw me as a person, a person with interests other than school and books.

Leaning back on my chair, I closed my eyes, my phone resting on my lap. When did things get so complicated? Probably when hormones got in the way of our relationship. That's when everything started to change, to get weird. Not a day had gone by where I didn't regret not doing everything I could to prevent us from falling apart.

I still remembered the first time hormones got the best of me. We were both twelve, and it was another normal school day. Still, to this day, I had no idea what triggered me so much. A newcomer entered the classroom, and he was inexplicably attractive as well as charming. He sat next to Aria…in my seat, and unfortunately, I'd been late that day, so by the time I arrived, he had already claimed my spot.

***

"Hey, I'm Xander, Xander Lee," he said as he put his hand forward to shake Aria's hand.

"Hi…Xander, I'm Aria, Aria Xing," she replied, accepting his greeting and returning her own.

That single handshake made my blood boil more than any experience I had felt before. I always sat right next to Aria, me. I had done so ever since preschool, and Jesper and Rosalie always sat close by. That wasn't supposed to change.

I wasn't sure what to do, but I felt extremely angry and insecure. Xander was leaning in close to Aria, too close, talking to her, and she wasn't even looking at me. Rage burning in my veins, I approached them.

"Aria, why is he sitting in my seat?" I frowned in contempt.

"Oh, hi, Avery. I wasn't sure whether you were coming in today. Umm, Miss Rose told him to sit here since he's new. She suggested that I show him around," she replied gingerly.

"But you know I can't sit with anyone else," I whispered in her ear, my voice shaking with anxiety when I heard footsteps come up behind me.

"Sup, dude," Xander interrupted us, oblivious to the heated conversation.

"Avery, say hi to our new classmate, Xander," Aria said, still frowning at me, like I was the one in the wrong.

"Hey, Xander," I said, rudely, waving him off like I clearly didn't care about getting to know him. "Now, can you please sit somewhere else? That's my seat. There are plenty of other desks for you to choose from," I continued to insist.

"Avery, calm down," Aria chastised. "Just let him sit here! Be nice; you can find another seat!"

Too annoyed to even reply, I turned around and walked away, cursing under my breath.

"What the hell? He's in *my chair*, I wanna punch him," I murmured as I found an empty seat behind Jesper.

"You're in such a bad mood. What happened up there?" Jesper asked me.

Normally, I wouldn't respond to Jesper as we never really got along, always butting heads with our different opinions and the disgusting way he would stare at Aria, but man, did I need to rant.

"That damn Xander, for god's sake! He took my seat. I hate him!" The words escaped through my lips before I could reel them back in.

"Come on, dude, he's a newbie. Let him have his moment. Are you… jealous he's gonna be best friends with Aria, steal your girl away?" Jesper joked, a huge grin appearing on his face.

He was always joking and always grinning. Most of the time, especially when I was already furious. It made my blood boil even more.

"Come on, not now…" I peered at Aria, her long hair covering most of her face from where I was sitting.

"Are you staring at them? Man! Take a chill pill," Jesper said lightheartedly as he looked back at me.

To everybody's surprise, another new student entered the class a few minutes later. She was a wide-eyed Caucasian girl with dark brown hair and was taller than most of the girls in the class, taller than me even. Her big brown eyes were apprehensive of the new crowd as she stepped in. I distinctly remembered everyone staring in awe.

Being in a school surrounded by Asians, it was a surprise to us all to encounter someone of a different race. We were all so used to our little pocket of familiarity that we weren't sure whether we'd even get along with someone new.

"May I come in, ma'am?" she asked in a soft voice, addressing the teacher.

"Yes, you may," Miss Rose said in response.

"Thank you, ma'am."

As she walked towards the back of the room, all eyes turned to follow the new girl. She looked around shyly and picked the seat next to me.

"Hi, I'm Jess," she murmured as she sat, her cheeks pink and hot.

"Hey, Avery," I replied, my heart skipped a beat as I made an effort to plaster a welcoming smile on my face, my face still beaming red.

"What are we learning? I'm new here," she whispered.

"Geography, do you have the textbook?" I asked her as gently as I could.

"Umm… nope. I didn't know I needed it. No one told my mom that I needed to come prepared," she admitted with a little shrug.

"No worries. Happens to all of us. Here, you can share mine."

As I smiled at her, she winked back, and suddenly, I soon forgot about Aria and Xander.

***

Fading back to the present, I relinquished the memories of the past as I kept on scrolling through the pictures. Memories, such a brittle thing, but at the same time, so vivid. Looking at pictures of the past was like drowning in an ocean of flashbacks where the beauty of the memory is inexplicably magnificent.

Because the truth was, we usually only recall the good.

Chapter Three

Hi, my name is Aria Xing.

I always considered myself to be pretty unusual, strange and freaky, as most would call me. It's not that I'm weird, but more that I never felt like I could really fit in anywhere. My vibrant and bold personality attracted people to me just as quickly as it would chase them away. But I didn't care. I knew who I was as a person, and I wasn't about to change that for anyone.

However, it was that same mentality that had left me alone year after year.

When I graduated college, it didn't take long before I realized that I didn't belong in my hometown. I took a mediocre job in Los Angeles and was down in the dumps for a while, sleeping with random men just to feel a sense of excitement in my life. But I eventually picked myself up. I usually got what I wanted in the end, my ambition never letting me down despite who I hurt along the way.

I was a taker, not a giver, and selfish as it may be, I didn't care.

But none of it mattered in the end, because I always found a way to fuck everything up. Has been, and always will be. As I walked quickly through the streets of Los Angeles, my phone rang.

"Hey, Aria, you up for another night of fun?" Jesse, my hookup from last night, asked on the other line.

Without saying a word, I rolled my eyes and hung up. Last night was a mistake. I had a little too much to drink and jumped into bed with the first guy who touched my hand. I didn't even know what he looked like until I snuck out of his room this morning.

Why do I always get the creeps, the degenerates? Why don't the good ones ever call me back?

I was beginning to get tired of these one-night stands. I just wish I could settle down with a husband and start a family, the whole ordeal.

As I hung up, I looked at the messages on my phone. The text I had sent Avery over two weeks ago was still there, unanswered. Seen, but unanswered. It had been years since we last spoke, and I wasn't sure what exactly triggered me to text him after so long. Maybe it was my birthday and the sense of time that brought with it. Maybe it was all the excessive alcohol I had been drinking lately to forget about my problems.

Or perhaps it had been running into Rosalie last month, who looked at me like I was a failure, like I had fucked up. We used to be so close; now, we barely speak as I was pretty sure she hated my guts.

And she had a point. Perhaps the first time I fucked up royally with Avery, was when I turned thirteen years old.

***

That year, I had my first ever surprise birthday party. I remembered coming home to an unusually dark house, and the lights suddenly turning on as I walked in, party bombers rumbling while everybody yelled, "Happy Birthday Aria!"

It started as one of the best days of my life. I had on an ivory strapless gown, my hair up in a French bun, and just a little bit of makeup on. I felt like a queen, glamorous and amazing, and I should've known the surprise was going to be at my house, but my mom had completely fooled me into thinking we were going to pick up a cake and then head to a restaurant. Everybody praised my beauty, the dress, and the party was filled with fun and games.

When I finally got to cut the cake, red velvet with cream cheese frosting, my favorite, a lot of pictures were captured, and I was engaged in the hustle of the crowd again.

"Hey, Avery. Lost in your head again? Buckle up, dude. It's a party!" I heard Jesper say close by, turning my attention to my closest friends.

"Umm… nothing. I mean, I'm fine," Avery sighed.

"Hey, man. Tell Aria I'm leaving. It kind of blows here. Rosalie's coming with me too. We're going home and playing video games," Jesper said. "Rosalie, let's bounce!"

"Cool, see you later," Avery replied, distracted.

One by one, I saw my friends vanish swiftly until it was just Avery and I left. It had been a while since we'd last hung out, especially since we weren't on good terms ever since Xander came into our lives, so I asked him to stay.

My parents told me it'd be alright for him to stay for a while and headed off to bed as they had to be up really early the day after to go to work.

"Aria, I should get going. Mom's probably still up waiting for me," Avery murmured while looking down.

I could tell there was still tension between us as he refused to look me in the eyes.

"Come on, Avery, no. Please. I miss you. We've been so out of touch lately, and I don't want our friendship to fall apart," I begged in an alluring voice.

"But…" Avery murmured, looking up at me. "I…I can't…"

"No buts. I wanna have some fun on my thirteenth birthday. Please stay," I continued to beg, this time, with a little pout.

I secretly knew that would always be my special weapon to get Avery to do what I wanted. Of course, I'd never tell him that. I couldn't lose the little servant I had. It was too much of a good thing. Race me to school, jump over the neighbor's fence to get my ball back, jump the line in the cafeteria to snag me the last piece of lemon meringue pie, and even lie to his parents so he could come over and stay until later than he was allowed to.

"Uh…alright, fine," Avery finally gave in after several minutes of silence, looking up at me between his lashes.

"Thanks! You're the best!" I cheered joyfully, embracing him in a tight hug.

Avery's cheeks turned red as we hugged, and he looked flushed, but I ignored it as I pondered what to do next.

"Okay, let's do something exciting. It's my birthday. We should do something EPIC! Something to remember forever. What should it be? Any ideas?" I asked.

"What kind of… exciting?" Avery asked nervously as he knew I always had the craziest ideas that would get us in trouble.

"Oh, I have an idea," I said as I suddenly remembered a conversation my older cousins had a few days ago.

"Let's drink some wine! I know where Mom stores her stash," I said excitedly.

"Are you kidding me? We're way too young," Avery countered, stunned.

"Avery, don't be a pussy," I said with a frown. "My cousins told me it's a lot of fun, that it makes you feel… things," I finished, not sure how to explain.

"It's not being a pussy. Your mom's going to kill us if she finds out," Avery frowned back at me, crossing his arms over his chest.

"Nah, you're just being paranoid. She's never going to find out. It'll be our little secret, just between us," I said convincingly. "She's got way too many bottles to notice one missing, and I'll make sure to make the evidence disappear," I added, a plan already sorted in my mind.

"This isn't exciting at all," Avery rolled his eyes.

"Avery...please!" I pleaded with my eyes, hoping he'd fall for it.

My friend scowled, so I pouted my lips again.

"Ugh, why do I always let you talk me into these crazy ideas of yours? You're insane. Where do we even find her stash?" His voice was a resigned whisper, and it almost made me laugh.

"Yes! That's more like it!" I smiled widely as I silently walked towards the hallway. "You sit there, I'll steal it, and be back in a sec," I whispered over my shoulder.

"Roger that," Avery replied in a whisper of his own.

I silently snuck down the hallway before proceeding to the basement, went into the dark cellar, opened the door as quietly as possible, and grabbed a bottle of red wine from a label I knew Mom had plenty of. Then, I went back to the lounge where Avery was standing, still waiting, just like I knew he would.

The night seemed so full of charm and charismatic warmth. I felt older during that moment when the alcohol coursed between my lips for the first time. I was only thirteen, but I felt like I was in my 20s. I could do things adults did. Now that I had my bottle of wine, I could start living my life. I felt unstoppable.

As I sat down on the floor, I realized I not only had my wine, but also a table full of unopened gifts. "Let's play a game," I suggested as I noticed Avery still reserved, fiddling with his thumbs.

"What kind of game?" Avery asked, hundreds of questions written in his eyes.

"We'll open the gifts, one by one, and drink a sip of wine if the gift doesn't suck... as a way to celebrate it," I explained.

"Okay, fine," he shrugged casually. I could tell he didn't have the strength to argue with me anymore. I had worn him down.

We started opening the gifts, analyzing them and making fun of each one, and how silly it was to still get crayons at the age of thirteen. Whenever I opened one that I liked, like a cool video game or a stationery set, we chugged some wine and cheered, our voices always just over a whisper to avoid my parents catching us in the act.

Soon enough, all the gifts were opened, all except for one, and I knew it was Avery's. He always decorated his presents with a racoon sticker; that was his signature. I was feeling a little dizzy and nauseous, but I liked how the alcohol was boosting my emotions, making me forget about my problems.

My feelings were circling out of control, and I was losing myself and wanted to explore all the things I was feeling. There was also another unknown feeling deep down. I felt like dancing, like letting my hair down and spinning in circles, and so I did. I danced even though there was no music, and I let this weird sense of sexual energy wash over me as I swayed my hips from side to side.

I could feel Avery's eyes on me as I moved my body like never before, and I felt giddy, but also a little silly. As I sat back down, my head was spinning, and I giggled so much I thought I was going to wake my parents. I put my hands over my mouth, trying to keep quiet as Avery smiled at my childishness.

In front of me, I could clearly see that the wine had brought out a different kind of Avery also, one I wasn't used to, one I had never met before. The shy little boy I had known since I was a kid was gone, and as Avery took off his blazer and spun around in a circle, looking like a male model, I giggled again.

"Wow, that's hot," I chuckled.

"Do I look hot?" he asked, his eyes gleaming. "Am I appealing to you?" Avery asked playfully, all his shyness gone out the window.

"God, don't be cheesy," I chuckled again and took another sip straight from the bottle, trying to drop the subject.

But Avery refused. He enjoyed the conversation we were having and wanted to keep going. He undid the top two buttons of his dress shirt and combed his hair back with his fingers.

"Is that hot? Am I turning you on?" he asked playfully as he moved a little closer to me, lifting his brows.

"Are you trying to intimidate me?" I asked, confused. "Stop it. Don't mess with my head… Let's... Let's just open your present," I stammered.

"Okay," Avery said, taking a step back, his eyes focusing again, but I could tell he didn't actually want to stop.

I was curious to open his present, as year after year, our presents to each other had always been really thoughtful and special. Two years ago, he wrote me a little book of poems about how much our friendship meant to him, and last year, he folded me a thousand paper cranes as a sign of good fortune and luck.

When I unwrapped it, I found a bracelet and a sketchbook inside, the same sketchbook I had given him for his birthday. When I opened the book, I found paintings and sketches of myself all the way from childhood until the present. There were tons of them. And the bracelet, it was the one I saw at the mall and had wanted so badly but couldn't afford.

"Oh my god! Are you kidding me?" I said, shocked. "This is so freaking awesome! I can't believe you got me my dream bracelet!"

"I'll take it as a compliment," Avery smiled, his body swaying a little.

"I love it. I love you, Avery," I said while turning the pages, still amazed by the drawings in there.

Little did I know, that was not the only time I would ever utter those words to him.

"I love you too," Avery's tone sounded intense, his words not nearly as innocent as mine had been, deep and full of feelings like they had been kept secret for so long.

I looked up at him, feeling confused.

"Do you really like it?" he asked, inching closer again.

He took my hand in his, and I saw the passion in his eyes. I had never been in a situation like this before that moment. Nervous, I pulled my hand back, unsure of what to do next.

"I think you're a little drunk. You're not acting like yourself," I said hesitantly. "Hey, Avery," I shook my hands in front of his face, "I'm Aria, your best FRIEND, remember? I just love your gift... that's it. Stop looking at me like that," I tried to fake a smile while also leaving some distance between us.

"I'm...fine. My feelings are just a bit boosted. I want to tell you something... really bad, something I wanted to tell you for years now," Avery said, leaning forward and getting closer again.

"Whoa, Avery, you are definitely wasted," I chuckled awkwardly as I inched away even more.

"Wow! What am I even feeling? I'm really heating up, like, I'm so hot right now…" Avery drifted off, undoing two more buttons of his shirt.

"Oh god, are you gonna puke? I think you had enough wine," I said while going over to him and putting my hand on the nape of his neck.

I gently rubbed my fingers down his back, the same way my mom did whenever I felt sick.

"Please don't tease me like that," Avery said, his eyes snapping up at me.

Before I could tell what his plan was, he forbade my hand, and then kissed the back of it, his lips sloppy.

"What the hell are you doing?" I snapped my hand back as I screamed, my words interrupted when Avery's lips found mine.

At first, it was a gentle and slow kiss, a mere touch of two soft lips, but gradually, it got more intense and more appealing. I found myself liking it, wanting more. After all, it was my first kiss ever, and the feeling of it caught me by surprise. All the nerves in my body seemed to turn on at the moment, and that's when the intensity of the kiss really hit me.

When I finally opened my eyes after that initial shock, Avery had his right hand on the nape of my neck, and his left hand was on my waist, pulling me towards him strongly. It was strange to see that the shy and introverted Avery could be so wild, aggressive, and romantic at the same time. His lips were still pressed over mine, and his tongue suddenly poked in between my lips, exploring the inside of my mouth.

I could feel his right hand brushing up and down my back as if he was trying to remove something before I pushed hard on his chest, and Avery staggered back.

"Avery, no, this isn't right!" I yelled at him even though I secretly enjoyed the kiss, and I tried to calm down, easing my tone so as to not wake up my parents who were still sleeping soundly upstairs. "You're wasted! You don't know what you're doing," I said, feeling utterly embarrassed.

Avery looked into my eyes and then down to my lips. He opened his mouth and then closed it again, as if he was unsure of what he could possibly say to make this situation okay.

"This wine is messing with our heads… you're my best friend, Avery," I muttered.

After several minutes of silence, Avery finally spoke, "It's not just the wine… I like…I like you, ever since I first laid eyes on you. I love you, Aria."

Avery's demeanor reverted back to his normal shy self, his gaze on the floor, his fingers fidgeting by his side, but words continued to escape from his mouth, words that I never thought I would hear him say.

"This is not like a best friend liking another best friend… I like you the way a boy likes a girl. I wanna be your… boyfriend. I want to give you the love you deserve and treat you like a queen," he confided.

"I don't get it…" I mumbled. "You're just my friend, my best friend. That's it. I don't think I can ever see you as anything other than that."

"Oh… well, we can still be friends! I just want more than that, and it hurts when I see other guys staring at you, especially Xander, knowing I can't do anything to stop it," Avery muttered, clearly hurt by my choice of words.

"I'm sorry, Avery. You can never be my boyfriend," I tried to explain softly without hurting him even more. "I just don't feel that way about you. I'm so sorry. We're friends, just friends," I said and took two steps back.

"Why not?" he sounded so sad that I almost wanted to hug him, but I knew this was definitely not the right time for that. "Can't we just give it a try? We're meant to be together, I just know it! Please, Aria, please say you'll be my girlfriend," Avery continued to plead.

"I just can't... I just don't see you like that. You're my best friend, please... don't ruin our friendship."

Avery stood up, grabbed his blazer, buttoned up his shirt, and gave me a disappointed look. "It's way past my curfew, I should go," and without saying another word, he left.

The night had started out amazing, just me and Avery enjoying life together, and it ended with me almost losing my best friend. A ruined memory by the stupidity of two foolish teenagers who thought we knew better than we did. Me, thinking I was mature and old enough to drink alcohol, and Avery, thinking he was in love with me and opening up his heart, only to find a version of myself that didn't feel the same for him.

***

Back then, I didn't know I was going to fall for him... hard. I didn't know I was going to become the jealous girl running after an old friend, wishing I could turn back time and take back all those nasty rejections I had thrown at him.

Little did I know, I was going to fuck up both his life and mine.

Chapter Four

The night after Aria's thirteenth birthday party, I woke up with a massive headache and throbbing back pain. I then heard a knock on my door, followed by my mom's voice.

"Hey, Avery, sweetie, breakfast is ready."

As consciousness grabbed me, I realized the mess I made the night before. I had fallen asleep on the floor wearing only my boxers, and I got up fast, my head spinning.

"Coming," I said quickly, my voice sounding raspy. I had a hangover before I even knew what a hangover was.

"Hurry up, Dad's waiting. He needs to go to work soon," she replied, and then her steps echoed as she went downstairs.

"No, no, no," I muttered. "Hell, what have I done?" I whispered as I looked at myself in the mirror.

I grabbed my clothes from the floor while trying to process what had happened last night, the disaster I had created, hoping I didn't lose Aria as a friend forever. I hopped into the shower with flashbacks of kissing Aria.

It was an amazing kiss, everything I ever fantasized it to be and more, but then… then she smashed my dreams and knocked me down. She didn't like me, like… really like me. Not the way I liked her.

I made such a fool of myself. I thought I had ruined our relationship forever. When I finally got downstairs, my mom looked at me with concerned eyes.

"Darling, you came home late last night. I know it was Aria's birthday, and her mom called me, but you know we have an agreement. No staying out past 10pm," she reproached me.

"He's becoming a man. I think it's only natural if he wants to stay out late. You don't have to protect him so much, honey. He's not a little boy anymore," Dad interjected before turning back to his morning paper.

"Sorry, Mom," I murmured, still lost in another realm of emotions and fantasy.

"Avery… Avery," she called again and again until she got my attention.

"Yes, Mom?" I asked, and then sat down in my seat as Dad sipped his coffee.

"Are you okay, honey? Is everything alright?" Mom asked anxiously.

"Yeah, Mom. It's just a headache. I'm late for school; I should get going…" I grabbed my backpack and turned towards the door.

"Honey, wait, I'll give you something for that headache…"

"Mom, I'm fine. Don't worry. Bye, love you," I quickly interrupted as I walked out and grabbed my bike from the garage.

"Bye, honey…" Mom called after me.

Normally, I'd meet up with Aria before biking to school together. We had been doing so for years, but today, I woke up late, and Aria had already left for school when I went past her house. Plus, I wasn't sure I was ready to face the embarrassment of coming face-to-face with Aria.

I felt such shame, and I didn't want her to see me like this as she usually saw me as strong and composed, not the idiot I had portrayed myself to be.

Going to school alone made me rethink my impulsive attitude from the night before. I was so sure I had ruined my relationship with her forever. All I could remember her saying, over and over, was, "I don't like you, Avery, and I never will." That broke my heart.

How could I have been so stupid? But… why was what I did so bad? All I did was express my true feelings, so why was I feeling like crap? I knew I was a little drunk, but I told the truth. I told Aria exactly how I felt, like friends were supposed to tell each other.

Why was that such a bad thing? Was it really that wrong to have feelings for my best friend? I didn't think it was. But maybe that was the problem, that I felt a certain way towards her when she didn't feel the same towards me no matter how much I begged.

Or maybe, she had said those things because she didn't want to admit how she really felt for me. Maybe she really wanted to be with me too but was just too afraid of losing our friendship in case something were to happen that tore us apart. Maybe she was too shy to admit she liked me. After all, she had been pretty keen on the kiss when I first laid my lips on her.

She'd kissed me back, right? That should count for something. I thought that maybe when I got to school, I could apologize for the way I acted and start over. Tell her how I really felt, deep from the heart, while I was sober, explain my feelings, and wait for her to tell me she felt the same.

That would definitely work, right? I thought to myself the entire journey there.

The internal back and forth sure didn't help, and by the time I got to school, I was even more confused than before. The kiss had not only been special to me. I was certain that it had been special for Aria as well. Aria didn't back out at first, so she had to have also enjoyed the kiss.

When I chained up my bike and went looking for my friends, I was astonished by what I saw in front of me. Aria was chatting and laughing with Xander, her hand touching his arm like she was flirting with him, which made me instantly green-eyed.

I never liked Xander; he was always trying to get intimate with Aria, and seeing them like this now, right after the kiss Aria and I shared, I wanted to clock the guy in his stupid face.

Jesper and Rosalie were engaged in their own conversation right next to them, as always, so I approached the group.

"Hey, Jesper," I muttered, making effort to avoid looking at Aria as I knew my facial expression would give away my anger and jealousy.

"Hey, dude," Jesper welcomed me into a conversation to which I didn't feel invited.

"What's up?" I asked Jesper while glancing intermittently over at Aria.

Xander was holding Aria's hand, the other wrapped around her waist, and I didn't know what to think about that.

"Actually," Aria interrupted, having heard my conversation with Jesper. "Xander and I are planning on going to a movie after school. Xander said he wants to spend some time with me outside of school, and there's this kickass action movie that just came out. He's new to this town and wants a familiar face to show him around," Aria smiled while looking at Xander playfully.

"Yup! There's no better tour guide than someone as beautiful and sweet as Aria," Xander chimed in. "I'd be a fool to turn down a chance to spend time with her," he said with a wink, and then he kissed Aria on the cheek.

"Oh, that's cool. I hope you two have fun. Jesper and I are planning something too...something very, very special," Rosalie added as she pointed towards Jesper with a wink.

"Yeah, Rosalie and I will be busy this weekend, as usual," Jesper's tone was flamboyant, and I felt extremely left out and out of place.

It was supposed to be Rosalie and Jesper, Aria and me. Now, this fucking Xander kid was horning in on my woman and making me the third wheel. I tried not to think about it, about any of it, as I was burning with fury. Aria had a mischievous smile on her face as she quickly glanced at me, and I felt mine turn red.

"Aria," I said in agony, her name slipping off my tongue.

"Yes, Avery?" Aria smiled as she played with Xander's hair, making my chest hurt.

"I need to talk to you in private. Do you have… a moment?" I asked while staring down at the grass, rubbing my hands.

"Yeah, sure. Be right back, Xander," she replied, a small frown between her brows, as she gave Xander a kiss on the cheek.

We walked away from the group, heading toward the main building as the bell was about to ring. I kept rubbing my hands nervously, trying to gather my words.

"Um...so what did you want to talk about?" Aria asked hesitantly once we were out of the group's reach.

"I… I don't think you should spend time with Xander," I stammered while fixing the backpack on my shoulders and trying to keep my hands busy.

"Why not? Xander's a really good guy," Aria said with a confused frown.

"Aria… I wanna…" I stammered again, not knowing how to proceed.

"Avery, if you want to apologize for last night... I forgive you. The thing is, we *are* best friends. And everything that happened last night just messed everything up. I don't feel for you the same way you feel for me. It can never happen. And now, now that I know how you really feel, it's difficult for me to see you as a friend. Everything's just weird," Aria said in a flat tone.

"Aria, I know… you don't like me the way I like you. But maybe you should give us a try… Fuck Xander. He doesn't love you the way I do. We've been best friends for so long; it only makes sense that we're together," I stammered.

"Avery, I told you. We can *never* be together. There's no rule that says we're destined to be together. You aren't my type," Aria said, her tone now rising.

"Well…why didn't you stop me when I kissed you then?" I was getting angry again, my words slipping out of my mouth without my brain's consent. "Did you drown in the moment? I understand you don't want to be with me, but you didn't exactly push me away right away. I felt like you were enjoying it, just like I wa…"

"What the hell? What's wrong with you? Why would you think I'd enjoy it? I'm not even attracted to you. We're just…just friends!" She abruptly interrupted me, "I never thought you'd be this pathetic! That was my first kiss, a kiss I would have rather shared with someone who I didn't see like a brother. Of course, I'd act like that. I didn't know how to react! When I realized what was happening, I backed off," she replied fiercely. "I…I don't think we can be friends anymore, Avery. I can't keep having this conversation. I don't like you, okay? Get it through your head, and move on. Read my lips. We. Will. Never. Be. Together. Ever!"

I gawked at her, and Aria soon walked away. I felt tears welling in my eyes, the rejection making my stomach twist. All these years, I thought about Aria in such an idealistic way; she was my fantasy girl, the one and only love of my life. And now, all of a sudden, the glass dream castle was demolished within seconds, and all the high hopes I had for us were now flushed down the drain.

Aria was my whole world, and I felt completely lost and isolated without her in my life. I lost my closest friend due to one impetuous act. I was a jerk.

"So, you lost a genuine friend, your only friend. Great job, loser," a small voice inside my head kept repeating as tears dripped down from my eyes.

I shook my head, trying to shush the voice within.

"I love her…" I whispered.

I watched as Aria walked back to the group, and they all walked into the main building together, Aria snuggled in Xander's arms, leaving me outside on my own. The bell had already rung, and I knew I was going to be late, but I was rooted in my place, paralyzed, and unable to move.

We will never be together. She didn't really mean that, did she? We were so close, so similar and connected. Maybe she just needed some time to herself to think about us without me smothering her. Maybe she just needed to find her way back to me herself. Just…maybe.

I continued to wipe my tears with my sleeve as they trickled from my sockets. I had lost my best friend, and I would have to learn how to live without her... how to live a life without Aria, something I didn't even think was possible. I spent every day with her for almost the last decade.

She was my closest friend, my only friend. It was daunting just to think that I would no longer see her.

A dark and twisted life.

"Avery, are you alright?" Jessica Collins, the new girl, asked, showing up at my side. "The bell rang several minutes ago; we need to go inside, or we're going to be in big trouble," she looked at me intently, and I wasn't sure if she could tell that I had just been crying.

"Um...yeah. I just have a headache, that's all..." I wiped my cheeks with the back of my hand, trying to get rid of any stray tears.

"You should drink some water. That always helps me whenever I have headaches. Do you want me to get you some?" Jessica looked concerned, and that made me feel even worse for acting like a big baby, over a girl of all things.

"Thanks, but no thanks. I should just get going," I adjusted my backpack on my shoulders, unfolding the straps that were pressing against me.

"Okay, see you later then. I hope you feel better," Jessica smiled at me and gave me a hug before turning away.

"You too," I replied before walking the opposite direction.

***

Days turned into weeks, and Aria continued to ignore me, even when I tried to apologize and convince her that I was okay being just friends. Of course, she wasn't stupid. She knew me better than that. She knew I couldn't be just friends with her without wanting more. And she wasn't wrong.

My blood boiled every time I saw her hanging around Xander, the two of them with Jesper and Rosalie while leaving me out of the circle. I felt completely alone again, just like that first day when I met Aria. I blew it.

I had it all. I was best friends with the prettiest and most popular girl in school, and now, she hated my guts.

I started spending more time with Jessica, as she was the only person at school who didn't ignore me. She knew my story with Aria and was there by my side as I released my emotional rollercoaster on her. I felt like she truly cared about me, being there for me when Aria just ignored me for that…that asshole. I felt like Jessica was my only friend, and I was growing closer and closer to her.

"Hey, Avery," Jessica said one morning while we were hanging out in the school yard. "I have to tell you something. I like you…like really like you. Would you like to go out with me sometime?"

I was taken back when I heard those words. My whole life up until this point, I thought Aria was my one true soulmate. Never did I think I would be interested in anyone else, or anyone else would be interested in me. Plus, after the way Aria had made me feel, I thought I was unlovable.

Honestly, I didn't even really like Jessica. I never looked at her in that way. I never even thought we'd be friends; we were just too different. But she had been so kind, so sweet to me lately when everyone else couldn't be bothered with me, that I felt a strange pull towards her all of a sudden.

"Um…I guess? I mean, sure," I replied with such uncertainty that I was surprised she didn't just walk away then and there.

"Great! I'm so glad you said yes! There's a new action movie that's coming out this Saturday. I know you mentioned how that's your favorite genre. Would you like to go with me this weekend?" she continued to ask in her bubbly personality.

I paused for several seconds. I usually spent all my weekends with Aria, hanging out at the park or going out for pizza and ice cream. It felt weird to spend that time with someone else, almost like I was betraying Aria even though she was with another guy.

If Aria doesn't need me, then I sure don't need her.

"Sure, why not? Let's go to the movies together on Saturday. It's a date!" I exclaimed proudly as I pushed the thoughts of Aria out of my head.

As Jessica blushed red at my response, I felt myself more attracted to her. I didn't know whether those were my true feelings or if I was just so desperate to get Aria out of my head that I would've fallen for a tree in that moment.

***

Saturday finally arrived, the day of our date, and Jess and I met in front of the theaters. We lived on opposite sides of town so it didn't make sense for us to meet up beforehand. Plus, I didn't really want her knowing where I lived in case the date ended horribly.

After we got our tickets, I made a beeline towards the corridor as I usually did when I went to the movies with Aria. We both hated the idea of overpriced popcorn and made a deal to each other that we would never look in that direction ever again, blinding ourselves as we passed the station.

"Wait, Avery! Let's get some popcorn! We can't watch a movie without popcorn," Jessica called out and stopped me in my tracks.

It took me a minute to realize that this was no longer Aria, and I would have to be a good date and give Jessica what she wanted. With a sigh, I turned around and headed towards the refreshments with Jessica, spending over $10 on a small bag before proceeding to our room.

There goes my allowance for the week, I thought.

As we searched for empty seats in the crowded auditorium, I heard a familiar laugh behind me. I turned around and saw Aria and Xander, giggling and laughing with their arms embraced around each other. Fuming, I tried to turn away before they noticed me, but before I could, Xander called out, "Hey, Avery!"

I awkwardly and uncomfortably waved back while noticing that Aria was trying to hide behind Xander to avoid making eye contact with me. I then quickly grabbed Jessica and found some seats several rows behind them. I didn't want to be there, not while those two were there, but I also couldn't tell Jessica that *that* was the reason I wanted to leave. She couldn't know that I still had feelings for my ex-best friend.

I couldn't focus on the movie the entire time. Even though I had wanted to see it for months, I couldn't concentrate with Aria and Xander bonding right in front of my eyes.

How could she do this to me? How could she take nearly ten years of friendship and just crush it right in front of me, especially after knowing how I felt about her?

When Xander leaned over to kiss Aria on the lips, that set me off. That was supposed to be me. I became even angrier when Aria wrapped her arms around his neck and kissed him back, repeatedly, almost like a "fuck you" to my face. Rage overwhelming me, I reached over next to me and kissed Jessica on the lips, hoping Aria would notice and get jealous.

The kiss was nowhere near as special as the kiss with Aria, but I wanted revenge for what Aria had done to me that I couldn't think logically.

Jessica kissed me back with such passion that I immediately knew I had fucked up. Jess was clearly into me, and that kiss enforced that I was into her too…even though I wasn't. I wanted to make Aria jealous, but it didn't even seem like she paid attention, her eyes only focused on Xander.

Soon after, Jessica and I went on more dates, kissing whenever I saw Aria close by, and I started to notice how obsessed she was becoming with me. I knew deep in my heart that I didn't feel the same way for her, but I had used her so much to try and make Aria jealous that I didn't want to break her heart.

***

Six months passed by like the blink of an eye, and I still found myself missing Aria. I still craved her. By then, I was certain Jessica was falling for me. I even heard her whispering "I love you" to me several times, but I pretended not to hear. She had a very bold and tomboyish personality, a definite extrovert and nothing like me.

Aria and I had so much in common while I struggled to stay connected to Jessica, like we're always on opposite pages of the same book. Nothing like Aria.

By this point, I knew Aria and Xander were going steady, calling each other boyfriend and girlfriend, and I knew all hope was lost for me. Whenever I tried to approach Aria, Xander would stand in my way.

"She's *my* girlfriend, dude. You need to back off. She doesn't want you," Xander would always say to me, making me feel even more alone.

There were times where I caught Aria glancing over at me, and I could tell that she secretly missed me too, but things between us were just too complicated. I missed her every day, and I secretly drew sketches of her whenever I could. Whenever I remembered what she looked like. Whenever I could sneak a good enough peek to draw her with perfect details.

Sometimes I hated myself for ruining our friendship... I could've spent my whole life with just that precious bond of friendship, but I had to get greedy and couldn't leave good enough as is.

***

I miss you, Aria, I whispered to myself as Liana's name appeared on my phone.

Chapter Five

Aria's Story
Conflicted Feelings

After all the drama with Avery, I didn't know how to act around him anymore. And that's why I kept my distance. I still wanted him as a friend. I didn't want to lose that special bond we had, but things had just gotten too weird between us. We had been Aria and Avery for so long, best friends, our names always next to each other in every sentence, and now, we weren't even speaking to each other.

We grew further and further apart during the last half of that year, and I started to spend most of my time with Xander instead, and sometimes, with Jesper and Rosalie, who were dating by then. I could've sworn they dated even in preschool. They were inseparable.

I still loved Avery as a friend. I really did, but I never thought about him romantically. I just couldn't picture us together. I didn't want romantic feelings to ruin the good things we had going for us. I was so conflicted between my feelings that I even decided to stay quiet about his confession.

I started dating Xander by the end of middle school, and though I found him attractive, I never really got along with him the same way as I did with Avery. He was just always so egotistical and full of himself while Avery was humble and kind. Xander would argue with me whenever I said something he didn't agree with while Avery was more understanding to my needs and opinions.

When I saw Avery with Jessica at the theaters, I wanted to talk to him so badly. I missed his friendship and had so much to catch up on. But I knew I couldn't because Xander would get jealous as he always thought I had feelings for Avery even though I never told him what happened between us. I also wanted to warn him about Jessica as I heard not-so-great rumors about her from the school she transferred from, but I knew it wasn't my place to do so.

Avery was with someone else now, and I didn't have the right to ruin his happiness, despite what my opinions were.

When high school started, it didn't get much easier. Avery, Jesper, Rosalie, and I all went to the same high school together, along with Xander and Jessica. The whole gang was still together after all those years. After all that time apart in middle school, I wanted to hang out with my friend Avery, but my ego never allowed me to do so, the desire remaining only in my head.

Even if I didn't have romantic feelings for him then, I was somehow addicted to his innocent smile and his calm and composed personality. He was a huge part of my life, and he had a really special place in my heart.

Deep down, I wanted Avery back in our group of friends, for things to return to the way they used to be, but there was also a part of me that wanted him to apologize first. Over and over again until I could forget about what had happened.

During the first day of high school, the gang was once again reunited, and I was secretly happy that Avery was there, even if I couldn't admit it. I was still ashamed of my behavior but too proud to make the first move.

"I'm glad we all decided to go to the same school," Rosalie said happily after we all greeted each other.

The greetings between Avery and I remained tense and weird. We had spent every summer together ever since we met, and there was a hole missing in my heart without him. Xander was nowhere near as special as Avery; all he wanted to do all summer was play video games with his friends, leaving me to spend time all alone.

"Yeah, but those muscle heads over there are gonna find a way to do something to us, something bad to haze us," Jesper replied while gesturing to the senior jocks with his head.

For his usual cheerfulness, he seemed nervous.

"God, you're such a pussy," Xander chuckled.

"We'll see who the real pussy is when they come kick our asses," Jesper replied with a scowl.

"Stop it, guys, not now," Rosalie yelled, looking around nervously. "What if they hear you?"

"Hey, Jess, how are you doing? I haven't seen you around all summer," I asked with a mischievous and envious smile, interrupting the argument.

I couldn't care less about Jessica, really, I was just hoping I could get some information on Avery without having to directly speak to him myself. God, I so wanted Jessica to be miserable. I hated her guts for taking my friend away.

I couldn't stop looking at Avery while I spoke. He was still avoiding these too-personal situations, and now, he was glaring at the sidewalk while fixing the straps of his bag. He always did that when he got nervous.

"I'm doing good, thanks for asking," Jessica replied with a smile, always the polite one. "So, you and Avery used to be really good friends? He always talks about you," she added.

"Uh, yeah, we were…for a really long time," I replied while biting my bottom lip.

I wanted to scream at her for being with Avery even though I knew I deserved it.

Avery was visually distressed, sweating while his neck and face were getting red. He was clearly conflicted between his two lovers, unsure of whose side to take.

"Aria started hanging out more with… Xander, and I started hanging out more with you. That's how we drifted apart…" Avery stammered, still sweating and holding onto the straps of his backpack. "We just made new friends…" he said in a meek voice.

"Avery, are you alright?" Jessica asked, turning to him and looking concerned. "You're sweating bullets over there."

"Umm, yes, it's just hot here, that's all," Avery pretended to smile, but it turned into a weird half-smirk.

"Are you two friends?" I asked, interrupting and directing my question at Jess.

"Dating, actually. Avery is my boyfriend, has been for a while now. We're actually really close, like really, really close. In fact, he popped my cherry just this past summer. It was such a magical moment. Now, we have sex like every day," Jessica replied pleasantly while looking at Avery, her eyes shining bright.

"That fucking slut. We're only 14, and she's already fucking my best friend," I said under my breath, too low for anybody to hear.

We were so busy talking and catching up that no one noticed a group of seniors inching closer toward us. As I mumbled my answer, the seniors glanced over and then walked straight toward us, their tall bodies towering over all of us, even Xander, who was already 5'10.

"Hey, beautiful, I'm Tyler Morton. You may have heard about me, captain of the football team," one of them said to me with a smirk while playing with my hair.

"Hey, dude. Back off my girl," Xander stammered, turning his body slightly to get in front of me.

"Oh yeah? And what if I don't?" Tyler laughed at Xander, his friends mimicking him in the back.

"Um, I…" Xander murmured at a loss for words, his shoulders drawing in.

"You are a really beautiful girl, so hot and sexy," Tyler said again while inching closer, completely ignoring Xander now.

I looked over at Xander, shocked that he wasn't standing up for me. He was all talk and no action, and I couldn't believe that I was with such a coward.

"I…I have to go," I whispered quietly without making eye contact, trying to escape his wandering fingers.

However, as I tried to walk, Tyler reached out a hand and grabbed me.

"Where do you think you're going? We're only starting to get to know each other."

His grip was tighter now, and I was tired of not getting my way. I was already pissed at Jessica, and now this?

"Get your hand off me, now!" I exclaimed.

"Feisty little one, aren't you?" Tyler chuckled again as my face turned red. "Well, thing is, I don't like feisty," he said as he leaned in closer to whisper in my ear. "Welcome to high school, princess. I'm the top dog here, and whatever I want, I get."

As I struggled to get away from Tyler's attempted kiss, I heard a comforting voice.

"Let her go."

Everyone stopped and turned towards Avery. He was the last person any of us would expect to stand up to the bullies, and he was clearly terrified for his life but continued to defend my honor nevertheless.

"Just let her go."

"And who the hell are you? The second boyfriend? Standing up for your girl when that pussy over there is too scared to do it himself?" Tyler pointed over at Xander as he towered over Avery's small frame. "What are *you* going to do about it? You're scrawny as a rat," he mocked Avery as he gripped tighter onto my skin.

I could feel a tingling sensation of pain as the sweat continued to build.

"I said, let her go!" Avery was furious.

I could tell he had pent-up rage building inside him for a while now and was just waiting for the right moment to set him off. I watched as Avery pulled me loose from Tyler's grip and shoved him to the ground before the bell rang.

"You're lucky this time, punk. But watch your back. You'll regret what you just did," Tyler pushed Avery back before blowing me a kiss and walking away.

"Avery, let's go," Jessica said nervously after watching the whole exchange in a panicked silence.

It was clear that she was uncomfortable with Avery coming to my rescue.

Avery released my hand and didn't even look at me before leaving with Jessica. I had never seen Avery so furious before; he protected me with such courage, something Xander wasn't even able to do, and I had to admit, I was impressed.

Xander. Why the hell didn't he come to my rescue? Some big man he turned out to be as I came to my senses and saw the bitter reality.

"Xander, can I ask you something?" I asked as we walked to class, still perplexed by what had happened. "Why didn't you stop him? You saw him hurting me and trying to make a move, and you just stood there, frozen."

"Babe, what are you talking about?" Xander asked, baffled. "Oh, you're talking about Tyler Morton? He's not a bad guy; he was just messing around. Don't take him seriously."

"I think it was wrong... I think you were too scared to stand up for me," I confronted him.

"Babe, you misread that whole situation..." Xander muttered, but I turned on him and snapped my hand back, walking faster to get away from him.

That whole drama made me think about how I had purposely isolated Avery from the others, and how it was all my fault that he had almost no friends during the last six months of middle school and throughout the summer. I felt guilty, nonetheless.

Aria Xing, always fucking everything up.

***

About a month later, the drama began to settle down, and we all got ready for the Homecoming Dance. Xander and I made up and decided to go together since we were already going steady. Jesper was going with Rosalie, and of course, Jessica with Avery.

When I arrived at the venue and saw Avery in his turquoise-colored vest and bow tie, I couldn't help but stare. He looked inexplicably handsome in his black tuxedo.

Next to him, was Jessica, wearing a low-cut maroon off-shoulder mini dress and black heels, indistinguishable from a stripper. But she had it all when it came to appearance. Her body developed much quicker than the rest of the girls, and she had enough curves and cleavage to fill in her dress. No wonder Avery was so quick to jump into bed with her.

I looked down at my own outfit, disappointed with my flat chest beneath my long halter dress that looked like it hung off a coat rack. Xander matched me with his black turtleneck and an equally dark suit. He was nowhere as stunning as Avery was.

"Hey, man," Jesper greeted Avery as they stood to one side. He was wearing an Adriatic Sea blue suit with a soft pink shirt. "Jessica, looking hot," he added with a smile.

"Thanks, Jesper. Where's Rosalie?" Jessica replied as she blushed, squeezing her arms together so her bosom became more prominent.

"She's in the bathroom. Freshening up. You know, girl stuff," he smirked.

"I'll go see how she's doing, maybe get some pointers on what to do with these straps," Jessica said as she passively pulled the straps of her dress even lower than they already were, flashing a wink and blowing a kiss towards Avery.

As Jessica walked away, I could feel Avery's eyes on me. He smiled as he stared at me from top to bottom, and then his eyes stopped on the spot where Xander was holding my hand.

"Hey, Aria, you look really pretty tonight," Avery murmured reluctantly.

"Thanks, Avery. You look really good in that suit," I replied. There was definitely an unspoken sexual tension between us that neither of us wanted to admit.

Before either of us could say another word, Jessica returned, her brows low in a stern look as she saw the two of us talking.

"Aria, Rosalie's asking for you," she pretended to smile, but I knew she wanted to slap the shit out of me. "By the way, you look magnificent," she added, the fake smile still on her face.

"But I just saw Jesper and Rosalie walk off together…" Avery interrupted.

"Avery! Let's dance!" Jessica abruptly changed the subject as she dragged Avery onto the dance floor.

The lights dimmed as Xander and I found ourselves next to Avery and Jessica. It didn't take long before Jessica saw her chance at sabotage and stepped on the skirt of my dress, causing it to tear at the waist. I was humiliated! How could she do that to me?

My face turned red as the rest of the school laughed at me and stared. Fucking Xander didn't even do anything to help or stop them, and right then, in that moment, I felt like I didn't have any friends. Jesper and Rosalie had gone off to do god knows what, and I couldn't count on Avery to be on my side over his girlfriend's.

I quickly gathered the torn fabrics of my dress when I felt tears well in my eyes, and I bolted out the door to call my mom to pick me up. However, right when I dialed her number, I felt a hand on my shoulder, and when I turned around, I saw Avery behind me.

"You okay?" Avery asked quietly as tears continued to pour down my face.

"Why her, Avery? Why her? Why did you have to choose that…that bitch?" I whimpered and sniffled, fulling knowing I looked like a mess.

"I'm sorry, Aria, but you rejected me, twice, and Jessica was there for me…I'm sorry," Avery tried to explain as he wrapped his arms around me to give me a hug.

His grasp was strong, and I instantly found myself melting in his arms. All the memories of us together and how happy we were came rushing back to me, and I couldn't be happier to have my friend back.

When he finally released me, I found myself staring straight into his eyes as he dropped his hand from the nape of my neck down to my back, and then lower to my waist. I felt the warmth in Avery's seductive eyes as he continued to stare at me

We were both standing under the clear sky and beautiful stars, and I knew he wanted to kiss me because I wanted to kiss him too. He brushed a strand of my hair from my face and smiled.

"I miss you," he whispered as he started to lean down towards me.

However, our moment was interrupted when Avery's phone rang, with Jessica's screaming and demanding voice calling for him as he answered it.

"I…I have to go," Avery apologized to me before letting go of my hands and running back into the building.

All I could do was stare in silence, rejected.

Chapter Six

"Hey, Avery! A few of us are heading to the mall after school. They're having a huge sale on CDs. I'm super excited to snag some beats from my favorite bands. You in?" Xander called out to Avery the next week during lunch as Avery approached our usual table.

"Um…sure, why not? I'm sure Jess would love to come too. She's obsessed with the mall and everything shopping," Avery replied. "How about Aria? Is she coming too?"

"Coming where?" I asked as I approached the table. "Sorry, I'm a little late. I couldn't get my locker to open. Those damn locks. I can never remember the codes."

"The mall," Xander answered. "Remember how we were talking about hitting up the sale after school?"

"Oh, right, I can't wait. I've had my eyes on a new CD player I've been desperately needing for years now since my parents can't afford to buy me a new one." The smile I had when I saw Avery turned into a frown when Jessica approached us.

"Avery! There you guys are! I've been looking all over the place for you," Jessica exclaimed as she gave Avery a wet kiss in front of all of us.

"I'm sorry, Jess. Hey, listen, we're all going to the mall after school. Huge sale. You wanna come?" Avery asked as he wrapped his arms around her.

"OMG, the mall? Yes, yes, and double yes! You always know exactly what to say to cheer me up," Jessica chuckled softly before giving him another passionate kiss.

I wanted to throw up. I felt my face and neck growing more and more red at Avery and Jessica's affectionate public display. I had once been the most important person in Avery's life, but things had changed since. Now, Jessica was his queen, and I was the forbidden poison in his life. I didn't hate Avery anymore; in fact, I found myself falling more and more in awe of him.

I didn't know whether it was the jealousy, or whether I really did find myself falling for my best friend. Even if we couldn't be together, he was special to me as a friend, something I struggled to live without.

But it was too late. He had grown intimate with someone else, and my chances had become slim to none. I was sure that any potential relationship I could've had with him had been ruined.

Jessica and Avery were getting closer and closer day by day, and it was obvious that Jessica was falling in love with him. It seemed like Avery had moved forward in life, forgetting all about me. Although we were all together again in the same group, things were different.

We didn't have the inside jokes we used to. We didn't ride bikes to school together anymore. We even avoided the family get-togethers our parents would always try to arrange. Things were just…so different.

Avery had someone who cared about him, someone who gave him what he wanted when I couldn't.

***

"Happy birthday, Jess," I said with a fake smile a year later during her 15th birthday party.

Of course, by this point, I still had eyes for Avery. I was still jealous of Jessica and was determined to get him back. I didn't even know why I was still with Xander. I hated the way he treated me and the way he ignored me, but no way was I going to let Avery and Jessica one up me with their relationship.

"Thanks…Aria," Jessica replied as she saw my outfit, my long legs and bare back shining beneath my red strapless dress.

I could tell she knew what I was up to. After all, it was pretty obvious to everyone except Avery that I was after him.

"Hey, Avery. How have you been?" I asked flirtatiously as I turned around to greet him.

"Hey, Aria. Wow, you look…" Avery started to say, glaring at me.

I could definitely tell that he was interested, the affection he used to have for me still there. And Jessica quickly noticed.

"Avery, can you check the zipper on my dress? I feel like it's slipping down, you know, with all that weight I've been losing. Not everyone needs to walk around looking like a hippopotamus…or like they ate a hippopotamus," Jessica interrupted him with a seductive voice as she glared daggers at me.

"Sure, honey," Avery blushed visibly and turned his attention away from me.

"Aw, that's so sweet. I wish I had a guy who would do that for me," Rosalie praised, standing only a few steps away.

"Guys, get a room. You're making me look bad," Jesper joked sarcastically next to her.

"Maybe we should," Jessica blushed with a wink at Avery as she murmured the words, loud enough for almost everyone to hear.

"Who's ready for some beer?" Xander interrupted the discomfort between everyone as he stormed into the party carrying two six packs.

"Awesome, dude! Let's get this party turned up," Jesper cheered as he walked over to give Xander a high five.

Xander tossed a few cans onto some ice before throwing a few others to the rest of us.

"Ooohhh, let's play Truth or Dare," Rosalie called out after a few minutes of everyone chugging their cans. "Alright, Jesper. Truth or Dare?"

Jesper thought for a moment, carefully mulling through his decision before saying, "Truth."

"Who do you think is the prettiest girl in school?"

"Aw, come on, babe. Why you gotta play with me like that? You know you're my one and only! However, I do have to say, Aria is a close second. That dress is really doing you justice tonight, darling," Jesper winked at me while Rosalie playfully punched him on the arm.

"Aria, guess that means it's your turn," Xander smiled at me before throwing back his can. "Truth or Dare, sweet cheeks?"

"Um…" I thought for a minute. Normally, I'd choose truth as I was scared of embarrassing myself in front of everyone, but I was also afraid someone would ask me to reveal my true feelings for Avery. "Dare."

"I dare you to bring us more beer!" Rosalie chimed happily before Xander could even open his mouth.

"Are you insane? Honestly, I'm not even sure I can stand up right now without falling over," I frowned at her, my face turning blush red. The Asian glow was real.

"Don't be so dramatic. We need to keep this party going! Why don't you take Avery with you? He's the only sober one among us. Seriously, dude, how are you still sober?" Rosalie added.

"I dunno. I guess I can just hold my alcohol well. I think it's my genes," Avery stuttered nervously.

"Well, what are you two waiting for then? Get going!" Jesper shouted as he reached for another cold one, too drunk to even realize what was going on.

"Alright, fine. Come on, Avery. I know a shortcut…I think," I stood up and gestured Avery to follow.

"Bye, babe! I'll miss you," Jessica added as Avery walked over to join me.

Babe? I could barely contain myself. I wanted nothing more than to just scream at Avery for choosing that vile bitch over me, but I knew this wasn't the right time or place.

We walked around the streets for a while, unsure of where we were heading. I never had a good sense of direction, even when I was sober. However, I was very aware of Avery standing by my side. I could see him glancing over at me every few seconds, probably to make sure I didn't collapse.

I didn't care what the reason was. I wanted to be closer to him. I wanted him to want me and take care of me, to notice me. But the thought of him choosing Jessica still boiled in my veins, and I struggled with my feelings for him.

"Aria, be careful," Avery said while grabbing onto my arm as I slipped off the curb.

"I'm… fine. Just leave me alone, and go back to your damn girlfriend," I shouted, my voice fuming from out of nowhere.

"Aria, what's gotten into you? This isn't like you. You're sweet and kind and…" Avery started to say.

"Avery! I miss you, okay?" I interrupted. "I miss my best friend. We used to be so close, just us against the world. Now, we don't even speak anymore. We don't even look at each other anymore!" I could feel tears welling in my eyes as I spoke. I wasn't expecting all my pent-up feelings to just pour out at once.

"You do? You never told me you miss me. You've been spending so much time with Xander that I thought you moved on and replaced me," Avery replied innocently, his humility bringing back all the traits I loved about him.

"Well, I'm telling you now. I miss you, Avery. I more than miss you. I want you. I want to be with you," I finally confessed as I leaned in to kiss him.

I didn't know what came over me. Maybe it was all the alcohol, or maybe it was the jealousy, but before I knew it, Avery and I were locked in an embrace.

To my surprise, Avery didn't push me away. He pulled me in closer, like he had been expecting this moment for quite a while now. His lips felt like the first time we had been intimate, and a feeling of warmth surrounded me. I was in love.

Soon, our soft kiss turned into a more passionate one, making out with each other like we were starving, and the fact that we were both in separate relationships left our minds.

Avery turned me around and pushed me against the wall of a house, pressing my back against it. He kissed me harder, and then softly bit my bottom lip, sending shivers down my spine. I felt myself smiling as I kissed him back, my tongue exploring the inside of Avery's mouth as our tongues entangled in a dance.

When he slid his hands down to my waist, I relinquished my body to him and ran my fingers through his hair. Before I knew what I was doing, my fingers found the buttons of Avery's dress shirt, and I started to unbutton. He didn't stop me.

Instead, he ran his soft lips against my collarbone, across my shoulders, and down to my chest. I could feel my body tingling with every sensation. It did bother me that he was experienced, with Jessica of all people, but, in that moment, all I could think about was how Avery was mine.

As Avery continued to gently tease me with his tongue, a small moan escaped my lips for the first time, and it made Avery shift his hands toward my thighs. He spread apart my legs and glided his fingers along my inner thigh. I then felt his hands rising up my back to pull down my zipper, his fingers fidgeting with the straps of my bra, almost exposing my bare body before I suddenly took a step back.

"I can't, Avery. This isn't right. You're drunk. We're both dating other people, and we're outside someone's fucking house."

Avery looked ashamed by what I had said, his body shutting down by yet another rejection from me. He backed away, a cold feeling of loneliness engulfing my body by his absence.

"I'm…I'm sorry," he stammered as he quickly buttoned up his shirt and ran back to the party, leaving me all alone.

I didn't know what to do. I had hurt my best friend again and didn't even mean to. I finally had my chance with him, and I blew it, the weight of another mistake sinking me to the ground as I trailed behind him from a distance.

When I got back to the party, only Rosalie and Jessica were in the living room. Jesper had taken Avery out back to shoot some hoops while Xander ran out for more beer.

"Aria, come here, come here," Rosalie gestured to me when I walked in through the door.

"Sorry, Rosalie, I wasn't able to get more beer. Something happened, and I got sidetracked," I began to explain, careful as to not give too much away.

"It's okay. It's okay. Jess has something *big* she wants to tell us. Come, sit down," Rosalie rushed me over before turning her attention back to Jessica, who was turning bright red. "Well, Jess, what's the big news?"

"I…I think I'm falling for Avery. I think I love him," she spoke in a quiet voice as I felt my heart sink to my stomach.

"Are you sure?" I blurted out. "I mean, do you even know what love is?" I tried to correct myself when Rosalie shot me a nasty look. "Maybe your hormones are just throwing you off. I've known Avery for a very long time, since we were kids. I'm not so sure this is a good idea. You might ruin whatever good thing you have going for you. He's not really a relationship kind of person."

"What are you talking about?" Jessica asked defensively. "All he ever talks about is being with the girl of his dreams which, of course, is yours truly. Avery and I are PERFECT together. You're just jealous that he likes me and not you."

She was right. I was jealous. I had lost my chance, more than once. For the first time ever, I was genuinely afraid of losing Avery. Sure, he and Jessica had been dating, but love would bring their connection to a whole new level, one I wouldn't be able to compete with.

Although these last few years had been rough, that kiss with Avery drowned me into unidentified sentiments that I still wasn't sure how to act upon. As I sat there in silence while Rosalie and Jessica shared dating stories, I felt overwhelmed by the realization that I had lost.

I excused myself to the bathroom when I felt myself trembling with sadness. Standing in front of the mirror, I whispered to myself, "Get it together, Aria. You had your chance with Avery, and you blew it. You don't even know if you want him; you just don't want anyone else to have him. It's Jessica's turn now. Stop being a jealous little brat and move on."

But I couldn't bring myself to accept the truth. Avery and I had a special bond we never thought anyone could break. We were like two peas in a pod, connecting emotionally rather than just through sex and lust. He was like my other half, my twin with whom I could channel my thoughts to without having to speak.

But, on the other hand, I did reject him, causing him more pain than he needed. And Jessica cared for him the way I should've cared for him.

Maybe she is a better girl for him than I am.

Maybe it's selfish of me to stand in their way, even if there was a part of me who knew Avery still loved me. That kiss we had was undeniable, a moment I wish I could repeat on a loop.

After I calmed my nerves, I went back out to join the girls, right when Jesper and Avery were coming back inside, Xander walking in also with some more beer. I tried to let my worries wash away as Xander held me in his arms and gave me a hard kiss.

I could see Avery staring at us from the corner of my eye as Jessica walked over to embrace him. It didn't take any guessing to know that he was hurt, that he thought I had played him, broke his heart again by choosing Xander over him…again.

"Alright, guys. It's time for cake! Let's all head into the kitchen. There's a special surprise waiting for a special someone," Rosalie clanged on an empty glass with a spoon.

As I proceeded to walk towards the kitchen behind Xander, I felt a tap on my shoulder. I turned around, and it was Avery.

"Hey, Aria, can we talk for a second? Alone?" he whispered softly to avoid anyone overhearing. He then gently grabbed my hand and led me outside.

"Listen, I know you felt that spark between us because I definitely felt it too. I love you, Aria. I always have, and I always will. I never stopped cherishing that special connection we have between us. I know we're soulmates," he blurted out his confession as soon as we stepped onto the porch.

"Avery…I don't know. We're friends. You're with Jessica…" I started to speak, but he shushed me.

"I don't care about any of that. I don't care about Jessica. I don't love her. I love you. Just say the word, and I'll leave her in an instant." He grabbed my hands and held them close to him. I could feel his heart beating a mile a minute.

A million thoughts circled through my head. There was definitely a vibe between us, and I loved him just as much as he loved me. But I was scared. I didn't know what to do. I wanted to be with him, more than I wanted to be with anyone else.

So why couldn't I make up my mind? Why couldn't I just relinquish my fears and selfishness and be with Avery, like I wanted?

"I'm…I'm sorry, Avery…I can't," I finally whispered after a long silence.

And just like that, I saw his face fall, dropping my hands, and without saying a single word, he walked back inside.

I didn't know what was wrong with me. I had everything I wanted, and I just threw it all away. All that time of being jealous of Jessica, just to give it all back to her. I wanted to kick myself.

Why couldn't I say yes? Why couldn't I just be with him, like we both wanted?

As I walked into the kitchen, Rosalie was making a toast in honor of the birthday girl.

"Ladies and gentlemen! May I have your attention, please? My dear friend, Jessica, here would like to make a special announcement to a special someone."

I watched in horror and regret as Jessica stood up from her chair and walked over to Avery. She sat down in the chair beside him, grabbed his hands, and said, "I love you, Avery Cheung. We are soulmates, and I love you with all my heart."

"Oh damn! Avery's getting the L!" Xander teased as he nudged me with his elbow. I could only look at him with disgust.

Avery looked over at me for a second, hoping I would say something at the last minute to save him from Jessica, but I was at a loss for words. Disappointed, he turned back to Jessica and said, "I love you too."

I could feel my heart breaking as they embraced in a kiss.

"Aw, this is so romantic! I love *love*!" Rosalie smiled, taking a picture.

"Aria, are you okay? You look a little pale," Xander asked as he noticed me tensing up beside him.

"I...I need some air," I stammered. I pushed my chair back and rushed outside. I didn't just stop there. I ran and ran until I found myself back in the comfort of my own yard before collapsing into myself, tears streaming down my face.

Chapter Seven

It had been a while since the whole gang was together, and I had to admit, I missed my friends. But at least I still had Avery by my side. We were eighteen now, still madly in love with each other, and we both found universities close enough to each other to continue our relationship. I wished we could've attended the same school so I could keep him away from other college girls, but he was always the more intelligent one while I was more about physical survival.

Still, I knew we were close enough where I didn't have to worry too much about him cheating on me.

"Hey, Jess," Avery said to me one day when he knocked on the door of my dorm room.

We were supposed to spend the day at the beach. I just bought a new bikini and was excited to show off my body. I had been losing weight all summer and wanted to show off my success. However, the look on his face was a dead giveaway that the beach was no longer happening.

"What's going on? Are you okay?" I asked, looking disappointed already.

"I have bad news. Jesper's dad just passed away," he said.

Jesper Xi was one of my closest friends when I first moved into the city. He was always like a brother to me since he dated my best friend, Rosalie. But from what I'd heard, all four of them, Avery, Jesper, Rosalie, and Aria, were all friends since they were kids. I was the odd ball.

"Oh no, he must be devastated," I tried to sound concerned while still contemplating whether our beach date was still on. "We can go visit him tomorrow, or even after the beach, we'll stop by."

"They're actually having a mourning right now at Rosalie's. I came by to see if you're okay skipping the beach and heading over there instead."

I was pissed. I was looking forward to beach day for weeks, and now, it's canceled because of a stupid death that didn't even have anything to do with me? $100 saved up to buy this bikini, and now, no one was going to see me in it. Of course, I couldn't tell Avery. I couldn't tell him that I'd rather go to the beach than mourn his friend's dead dad. He would hate me. So, I sucked it up and agreed.

When we got to Rosalie's, Aria and Xander were already there. I forgot they were still dating. They had been on and off so many times that I never thought they'd make it, always arguing and fighting with each other. Rosalie looked the same as she had before, so did

Xander, but Aria, on the other hand, looked like a completely new person.

She had added highlights to her dark hair, cut her bangs, and started experimenting with push-up bras. She was also wearing a revealing black dress with heels while Rosalie wore something similar but with more coverage. I felt out of place in my pants suit, but it was the only thing formal I had in my closet at such short notice.

"Alright, great, everyone's here. We have to get going. The funeral starts in an hour." Rosalie started to gather everyone together as she ran down her checklist. She was always the most organized one out of all of us.

Funeral? I thought to myself. However, it wasn't like anyone could hear me if I spoke up. I didn't have a bold personality like Aria, and I didn't have the authority that Rosalie portrayed. I was just…shy. If I had known this was a funeral, I would've fought harder to not come. I was still planning on convincing Avery to take me to the beach after the mourning, but a funeral would eat up the entire day.

"Hey, Jess," Aria interrupted my thoughts as she tapped me on the shoulder. "Long time no see. How are you?" She gave me a hug, my arms wrapping around her perfectly-shaped body.

I always hated Aria, ever since I found out that she and Avery kissed during her 13th birthday party. Sure, they were both drunk, but Aria was everything I wasn't, and I was always afraid she'd steal him from me. He was mine. I didn't care how close they were, being the best of friends, but I'd be damned if I let her take him away from me.

"I'm good. Yeah, yeah, *Avery and I* are doing really well, so in love. We miss you. We all kind of fell out of touch after graduation," I tried my best to put on my friendliest face to hide my scorn, but I could tell that Aria wasn't buying it.

We both acted equally fake.

"Really? Avery, you missed me too?" Aria threw a flirtatious smile over towards his direction.

Avery was standing by my side, and he just gazed at her in admiration while raising an eyebrow. I felt a surge of anger inside me as I couldn't believe she was still after him. It was one kiss almost five years ago. Get over it already, bitch.

"Yeah, we BOTH did," I interjected before Avery had a chance to speak.

"Let's go! We're already late," Rosalie yelled from the kitchen, thankfully interrupting our conversation

"We can't yet. Xander just left to pick up the flowers, and he's not back yet. We can't leave without him," Aria said, turning her attention away from Avery's roaming eyes.

"Can you please call or text him or something? We need to get going. Jess, can you please help me grab some things from upstairs? Aria, since you have your license, why don't you and Avery load those boxes into the trunk of my dad's car and pull it around to the front? We'll pick Xander up along the way. We're running out of time as it is." Rosalie barely finished her commands before bolting up the steps.

Aria and Avery looked at each other in a way that I was very uncomfortable with. That should be me with

Avery, not her. It's not my fault I kept failing my tests; the instructors just all suck at testing.

"Wait, my phone. I left it on the couch. Let me go grab it. I'll be up in a minute, okay?" I lied to Rosalie when she led me upstairs.

"Fine, but hurry up. I need more than two hands for all this," she responded, slightly annoyed.

But I couldn't care less. Aria was trying to steal my man. No way was I just going to let that happen, not if I could do something about it. I waited until Rosalie was completely out of sight before I quickly darted out through the back door to the garage, hiding behind a large trashcan by the doorway.

I peeked over and saw Avery opening the door to the driver's seat for Aria before she climbed in, her eyes never leaving him. The shitty part was that his eyes never left hers either, their gazes so fixated on each other that I wanted to puke.

"Hey, Avery, can you help me with this? I think my seatbelt's stuck," Aria called out while pleating a strand of her hair behind her ear.

I watched in rage as Avery walked over and leaned over her to check the buckle, his teeth biting his bottom lip as Aria stared at him with her big brown eyes. I could feel the tension between them. I definitely knew something was going on.

I continued to watch, my heart racing faster and faster at the uncertainty. I wanted to jump out and scream at the both of them, for flirting behind my back, but then they'd know I had been watching.

After several agonizing minutes, I heard the buckle click, and Aria tilted her head back against the seat with her eyes closed.

"What's wrong?" Avery asked with his deep and soothing voice, the same voice that made me fall for him.

"Nothing, it's just hot in here. I feel like I'm suffocating a bit," she responded, her tone sounding like a victim.

I continued to watch as Avery placed his palm against her forehead to check her temperature, his fingers gliding across her skin before placing it back to his side.

"Are you sure? You look a little pale. Here, let's get you some fresh air. The girls can wait. We can't have our driver passing out on the wheel," he joked as he grabbed her hands and helped her out of the car.

Aria tripped as she stood up, and Avery was just the hero to catch her. He was supposed to be my knight in shining armor, not hers.

"Whoops, careful there. You almost cracked your skull." He gave her a quick hug before leading her out to sit on the porch.

If it wasn't for Rosalie blowing up my phone right then and there, I would've stormed out and confronted them. That was definitely not something "just friends" did. There was definitely something going on between them.

***

By the time the funeral was over, it was late, too late to go to the beach, and everybody was exhausted.

"Why don't we all stay here for the night?" Rosalie suggested when the group was together again.

"I can't. I promised my roommates I'd be back tonight. They tend to worry," Aria said straight away.

"Just call them and tell them you're staying over. I'm sure they'll understand. Besides, it's not safe to travel this late, and I don't want to leave Jesper alone during his time of need. There are enough rooms here for all of you," Rosalie insisted.

"But…" Avery opened and closed his mouth, and we all looked at each other for a moment.

"Stay for Jesper. He needs us, please!" Rosalie pleaded.

"Alright, alright. Fine," Aria was the first to agree.

"Sure," Avery chimed in right after, unsurprisingly. "Not like there's enough time to do any studying tonight anyway." He glanced over at Aria as she nodded.

"Fine," I answered also.

I really didn't want to stay, especially with Aria and my boyfriend in the same room, but I didn't want everyone to hate me by being the insensitive one. I just wanted to spend some alone time with Avery.

"Yay!! The whole gang is back together again! We should start a bonfire!" Rosalie cheered.

"That's a great idea! Let's do it," Xander celebrated with her. "I have a bottle of whiskey in my car. Let me go grab it. I'm sure Jesper needs something to take his mind off today anyway."

Xander gave Aria a quick kiss on the cheek before running towards the driveway. Rosalie also stood up to go grab Jesper from inside the house, leaving me, Avery, and Aria all alone.

Aria was the first to speak after a long and awkward silence. "Jesus, it's freaking cold out here. I wish we'd get that fire going already."

"Here, take my jacket. I don't mind the cold." Avery walked over and draped his jacket over her shoulders before sitting down next to her to keep her warm with his body heat.

At that moment, I remembered every time Avery and Aria had been together, and how Avery always went above and beyond to make sure that Aria was comfortable, doing anything and everything to help her in her time of need.

Sure, he was good to me, and he was a caring boyfriend, but whenever Aria was in the room, I always felt like I was the second most important person in his life, not the first. I knew what was going on; I could see the signs, but for some reason, I chose to ignore them.

After a few hours of sitting around the bonfire, Avery was still next to Aria, sipping whiskey and catching up on life. Jealousy peaked inside me when Aria rested her head on Avery's shoulder.

"Avery! Can you help me with something inside? I think I dropped my wallet somewhere," I yelled as I quickly stood up, startling everyone.

"Uh…sure," he responded before whispering to Aria that he'd be right back.

"It's getting late. We should all be heading to bed anyway." I heard Rosalie say as Avery and I walked away.

As soon as we went inside the house, I slammed the door shut and gave Avery a passionate kiss.

"Whoa, not that I'm complaining, but what was that for?" Avery chuckled. "I thought you needed to find your wallet."

"That was just an excuse to get you alone. I didn't bring my wallet. I just wanted you to come inside so I can do this," I said seductively, pushing Avery onto the couch and climbing on top of him.

I kissed him again, harder this time, and started to rip his tie off and unbutton his shirt.

"We shouldn't do this. You're drunk, and we might get caught," Avery hesitated as I continued to undress him.

"I don't care. I don't fucking care if we get caught. I want you, Avery. You're mine, and I want you so bad."

When Avery kissed me back, I glanced through the window and saw Aria staring right at us. Good. I wanted her to see. I turned my attention back towards Avery and proceeded to unbuckle his pants, pulling everything off until he was completely naked. It was late, and I was too tired for sex, but I needed Aria to see what I could do to Avery that she couldn't. I wanted her to be jealous of us, be jealous of me.

I slid my hands down his abs, kissing every crevice of his body and pleasuring him. I heard Avery moan as he undressed me and unclasped my bra, pressing his face against me and kissing my body.

"What was that?" Avery suddenly jumped when we heard a vase shatter.

"It's nothing, don't worry about it. Probably just something outside," I assured him. I looked up, and Aria was no longer there. She must've run away after seeing

Avery and I together, our naked bodies pressing against each other.

I climbed on top of him and rode my way to ecstasy as he touched me in places he had never touched before.

Avery was mine. All mine.

Chapter Eight

It was the night of New Year's Eve, and I was reunited with my friends once again at a banquet hall. We hadn't seen each other since the funeral four years ago, and I was excited to see them all and introduce them to my new boyfriend, Jovial Kora, a guy I had met online.

I was hung up on Avery for years, hoping that, one day, I'd get over my fears, and we could finally be together. However, that dream had died when I saw him and Jessica fucking the night of the funeral.

Xander and I faded out soon after that night. We never had much in common anyway, and he noticed that I was beginning to act distant so he broke it off with me to find someone who could pay more attention to him. I didn't blame him. He was an ass, but I wasn't exactly the best girlfriend either. We were both never meant to be together, just two young kids who happened to have a crush on one another.

"Hey, Aria, you ready to go?" Jovial broke me out of my thoughts as he called out from the first floor.

We didn't live together, but he was often over at my apartment since he still lived with his parents. I thought it was weird for a grown man to still live at home, but he was the only guy who I semi-connected with on the app, so I decided to give him a try.

Though, we didn't have much in common. I was into action movies while horror stole his heart. I loved to read non-fiction while he was more into comics. My dream was to travel the world with my two kids, and he didn't even want kids. But he was cute, so I guess that was enough?

"Coming!" I yelled back as I finished applying my makeup.

When I went downstairs, I could tell that he was agitated. He wasn't a very patient guy, but he forgave me when he saw me and gave me a kiss on the lips.

"You look gorgeous, sweetheart," Jovial said with a soft smile

"Thanks," I replied.

As we drove to the party, I couldn't help but become nervous at the thought of seeing Avery again. I had been avoiding him ever since that night, refusing to answer the many calls he had left me. I wanted to. I really did. I just didn't know what I would say to him without confronting him about that night.

I was with Jovial now, and I had to stop reminiscing about Avery. Jovial served in the army for a few years, traveling all over the world to countries like Bahrain,

Iran, and Afghanistan. I loved that he was fit and cultured, and I especially loved his Swedish and Russian background. Whenever he spoke, his accent would make me swoon into his beautiful green eyes.

He was the type of man any girl would fall for at first sight, which was why I found myself swiping right on him. But he was no Avery.

When we arrived at the party, my nerves revved up even more when I saw Avery, holding hands with Jessica. He was even more handsome than I had remembered, and she looked like she just had a recent boob job.

Sucking in my gut, I walked up to them.

"Hey, Avery, Jess. Long time no see!" I smiled as I gave both of them a hug, making Avery's especially long. "Meet my boyfriend, Jovial."

"Hey, mate, madam, pleasure to meet the both of you. Aria never mentioned she had such a gorgeous friend," Jovial smiled as he kissed Jess on the hand.

I didn't care, and it didn't seem like Avery cared either. We instantly locked eyes and refused to tear them apart.

"Aria, can I speak to you in private for a second?" Avery gestured to me as Jess and Jovial entered a flirting frenzy.

"Why didn't you ever pick up my calls? I know you got them. Not even a text? What's going on with you? I even went by your house a few times, but your parents told me you moved out. And who the hell is this tool? He looks and smells like he just walked out of a cologne catalog," Avery confronted me when we were out of sight.

"I…I'm sorry. I've been meaning to call back, but I've been so busy with work and Jovial, and I'm sure you've been busy with Jess, so I didn't think you'd care that much," I responded quietly. Avery was always a very soft-spoken guy, so whenever he raised his voice, I knew something was wrong.

"I call bullshit. Something's going on. Why are you avoiding me?" he asked again.

I couldn't keep it in anymore. Seeing Avery's face brought back all the painful memories I tried to push aside. "You really wanna know why?" I blurted out. "Because I thought we had something, something special, and instead, I found you ripping off Jess's clothes and fucking her at the funeral! That's why!" Tears poured down my face as my cheeks turned red. I had never been so angry at Avery or at myself for the way I felt.

Avery's face fell into a heartbroken frown when he saw tears roll down my cheeks. "Hey, Aria, I'm sorry you're hurt, but you specifically told me over and over and over again that we can never be anything more than friends. You rejected me more times than I can count while Jess treated me with nothing but love. What was I supposed to do? Just wait around for you until you decide to change your mind? God knows when the hell that'll be?" Avery was becoming defensive, and he had a good reason to, but still, I could not contain my tears.

I was beginning to make a scene, so he led me outside, and we sat on a bench by the gazebo.

"Aria, I'm sorry you're hurt. I really am, but I'm not going to apologize for having sex with Jessica. She is my girlfriend, after all. I knew we should've been more private about it instead of doing it on Jesper's couch, but I have needs too, Aria, needs that you didn't want to satisfy. Jess is my girlfriend, yes, but I've told you time and time again that I'd dump her in a heartbeat for you. But, instead, you decide to avoid all my calls and date this joker, flaunting him in front of me. What am I supposed to do?"

I didn't have an answer. I just sat there and cried. I was still conflicted over my feelings. Why was it so hard for me to just be with Avery? Maybe a part of me really didn't want him. Maybe I just didn't want anyone else to have him.

"Aria, tell me right now that you love me and want to be with me, and we'll leave here together, right now. No Jess. No Jovial. Just you and me. I still love you, Aria. Tell me you love me too, and I won't ever look at another woman again." Avery picked up my hands and held them tightly in his.

I remained silent. I wanted to tell him so bad, to just grab his face and kiss him on the lips, but I couldn't. I just sat there.

"Aria, be with me, Aria. Just say yes," Avery whispered, part of him already knowing what my decision was.

"I…I'm sorry," I finally spit out, more tears streaming down my face.

Disappointed, Avery dropped my hands and walked away, not saying another word. I wanted to slap myself across the face as I sulked on the bench. What the hell was wrong with me? I obsessed over and chased guys who were all wrong for me when the man of my dreams was literally chasing after me.

A few moments later, Jovial found me outside and sat down beside me.

"Hey, stranger. Why are you out here all alone?" he asked cheerfully as he kissed me on the cheek. "Come on, let's go in and dance. The party got started without you."

"Jovial, no. I can't," I replied as I pulled my hand away from his.

"No? What's wrong? Twist your ankle or something? Here, I'll carry you. I've lifted more than twice your weight before. This should be a piece of cake."

"Jovial, no, stop!" I spoke more assertively until he put me back down. "I mean, I can't do this anymore. I can't do this with you. I don't love you. I don't want to be with you. We need to break up." With that, I stood up and walked away, all alone once again.

When I got home later that night, I tried calling Avery to apologize and tell him that I love him. Breaking up with Jovial made me realize that I really wanted Avery, despite the fears I was feeling. I wanted to tell him everything I had been feeling for him and how I wanted to be with him for years.

I called and called, hoping he would pick up his phone, and we could meet up to share our first kiss as a real couple. Several rings later, no answer. I continued calling throughout the night, my excitement fading with each unanswered call.

He's not picking up, is he? I thought to myself as I finally gave up. I was too late.

I had spent all these years conflicted with my feelings. Now that I finally decided, it was too late.

A month later, I decided to pack up my bags and move to LA, leaving my painful past behind. I didn't want to live in a town that didn't love me back.

Chapter Nine

"You still love her, don't you?" Jess confronted me during the night of the New Year's Eve party.

Apparently, she had been watching when I confessed my love to Aria, holding her hands in mine and staring at her like I was lovestruck.

"I do," I whispered, ashamed. "But I told her, and she rejected me, several times, so now I'm done, done for good. I won't go back to her. I promise."

"I love you, Avery," Jess continued to speak. "I know I wasn't your first crush, and I know I can never replace Aria in your heart, but I gave you everything, and you *still* chose her over me."

"I know, Jess. I know. I didn't treat you the way you deserved, and I'm so sorry. But I'm done with Aria now, and I want to give us a fighting chance. I love you, and I don't want to lose you. I promise to never talk to Aria again. I promise with all my heart."

And I did keep my promise. Aria blew up my phone later that night, but I had to keep my promise to Jess. I screened her calls and promised myself that I would never speak to her again, for the sake of my relationship. She had fucked up my love life way too much for me to still be hung up on her. I was done.

***

Another five years had gone by, and Jess and I were still together. I spent most of my time working on my startup business while Jess found a great job as a financial advisor at a Fortune 500 company.

We were both doing pretty well for ourselves, a young power couple on our way to The Big Apple. We moved into an apartment together; the rent in the city was just so outrageous that it was impossible to not have a roommate.

Life in the city was going great, going out to bars every night and Broadway shows every weekend. Yup, everything was perfect, until it wasn't.

Soon, Jess began spending more time at work. It used to be that she came home at exactly 5pm every day, and we'd pop on the couch with a glass of wine while waiting for dinner to arrive. I still worked at home during that time, trying to build a career with my self-starter business.

But a few months after she accepted her new job, she began to come home later and later, several nights at 6pm, then 8pm, and soon her pattern turned into coming home close to midnight, always saying how her boss kept her late for some important project they had to finish for a big client.

I was used to being a loner, but I couldn't stand those nights home alone while Jess was still out there. I was constantly worrying that something had happened to her, that maybe she had been kidnapped or killed on her way home one night. The city wasn't exactly known as a safe town. I found my motivation beginning to diminish, as all I could focus on was what may have happened to Jess.

One night, while eating my Chinese takeout in sweats, I decided to pick Jess up from work. It was already close to 10pm, and if I really wanted to make sure she got home safely, the best option would be to go get her myself. It was late, and I had one too many drinks to remember where her office was.

As I drove around the streets of NYC, hoping to find a street sign to jog my memory of where to go, I suddenly slammed on my brake when I saw a woman who looked exactly like her. But she wasn't in her usual pants suits that she would wear for work; instead, she was wearing a tight, revealing club dress and high heels…locking arms with *another man*!

I didn't want to jump out of the car just yet; I wanted to see more in case my assumption was wrong. I'm not usually the type of guy to get up in someone's face and confront them. I always found it much easier and simpler to just walk away and leave it all behind.

So, I pulled my car over to the other side of the street and lowered myself to avoid being seen. Jess and this man, who was twice my height, continued to laugh and giggle. Her hands were all over this guy as he brushed aside her hair. I could feel my mind raging, reaching peak when the man leaned down and kissed her on the lips.

Foolishly, I was expecting Jess to stop the man, to tell him that she was in a serious relationship with a guy she lived with. She had always been loyal to me, and I didn't expect it to be any different.

But I was wrong. I stared in horror as she kissed him right back, wrapping her arms around his neck and pulling herself in closer. I wanted to storm out of my car and clock the guy in the face, but instead, I drove home.

Karma was catching up to me, and after all those things I'd done with Aria, I deserved this. Jess deserved someone better, someone who treated her with more respect than a guy who cheats on her with his ex-best friend behind her back. That night was a reality check for me, to finally snap out of my dream that if I just stayed with Jess long enough, then I would end up falling in love with her. It's been over a decade, and I found myself still longing for someone else.

During the long drive home, memories of Aria began to swarm through my head. I hadn't thought about her in years, assuming she's either still with Jovial or off to another man. She was never really one to stick to one guy for long, impulsively falling in love with men who weren't any good for her. I picked up my phone and scrolled through the history.

Aria hadn't called since the night I ignored her. She probably thought I didn't care anymore and gave up trying. It probably wasn't anything important anyway, probably just another one of her disruptive family stories. She always came to me for advice and support when her family was out of control.

Typical Asian family, I knew the feeling.

Pulling up her number, I was tempted to send her a message, to just ask her how she had been since we hadn't spoken in over five years. But I was ashamed that the minute I hear her voice or see her face, all my feelings would rush back, and I would confess my love to her again, leaving me with nothing but another rejection. I still loved her. I could never get her out of my head despite how much I drank.

Jess got home not long after I did. I quickly threw on my sweats when I got back and popped open a cold one so she'd think I was home the whole time. But I couldn't shake the feeling that we just weren't right for each other. She didn't get the love she wanted in a relationship, and I just didn't love her enough to care.

"Jess, we need to talk," I spoke quietly as she walked in through the front door.

She had changed back into her pants suit, probably so I'd think she had been at work this whole time. I wondered what other outfits she had stashed in the trunk of her car.

"Oh my god, Avery! You scared the shit out of me! I thought you'd be in bed by now. What are you still doing up? It's late, and you have that big pitch tomorrow," she said, flustered. I was sure she was just relieved that she didn't bring her boy toy home with her.

"Jess," I repeated again. "Are you happy in this relationship? Are you happy with me?"

"Happy? What do you mean? What's going on?" she replied, unsure of where the conversation was headed. "Hey, do we have any spaghetti left over from lunch? I'm starving."

However, I grabbed her hand before she could walk into the kitchen. "Jess, I think we should break up. You're clearly not satisfied with this relationship, and I've been in denial for too long. We're just not a good match for each other. Never have been, and never will be. It's time I finally face reality now. We don't have a connection. We're not good for each other."

Her face fell at my words. "It's about Aria, isn't it? You're still in love with her. After all these fucking years, you're still in love with that bitch, even after you looked me in the eyes and promised me that you two were over."

"No, this has nothing to do with Aria. This has to do with me. I thought that after we moved in together, I'd feel more connected with you and eventually fall in love. But that didn't happen."

Jessica was my first and only girlfriend. I didn't know how to break up with someone so I simply stared down at the floor, though, I could tell that she was tearing up.

"Avery…Avery, no, please. Please don't leave me. I love you. I love you with all my heart," she whimpered. "Please stay with me. I know we can make it work. I know we can work through this. We're soulmates, remember? Just you and me, forever!"

"Jess, no, we can't. We have to end this, now. You can keep the apartment. Our lease is almost up anyway. I'm going to find something closer towards uptown." I stood up and went into the bedroom to grab my suitcase. "Besides, if you ever get lonely, I'm sure you can just call up your side guy. I'm sure he'd be happy to see you again."

As I finished, I could tell that she knew I knew. She had been caught, and there was nothing for her to do but remain silent. After so many years of nothing but sex and lust, it was all finally over, and the silence between us was deafening as I walked out the door.

Chapter Ten

I thought moving to the city of opportunity was the best thing for me, a chance for me to start over, fresh. But, in reality, I only brought my problems to a new city. I was still confused and conflicted over my feelings for Avery. I wanted to move forward with my life, become successful in my career, but I could barely keep my personal life stable.

Dreaming about my goals and plans was a whole lot easier than actually living them to fruition.

Los Angeles was a whole new world, a world full of unseen truths and mystifying emotions. The first few years here, I struggled trying to live on my own in a town where I didn't know anyone. It was such an impulsive decision to just up and leave. I didn't even have a plan before I decided to drive across the country, working in fast food restaurants for nearly four years until I finally found a decent job in marketing.

All my friends back home were either married or had families while I was jumping from relationship to relationship, always falling for the ones who would inevitably break my heart.

After my last failed dating experience, I thought of Avery, how he loved me so much and was the one person who would never hurt me. I thought about how I had rejected him all these years just for him to no longer want me when I was finally ready.

He was the reason I left. I couldn't stand being in the same town as him and Jess, having them flaunt their relationship in my face. I never forgot that night, that night when I was so hopeful about us finally being together, just to have karma smack me across the face.

I had never been rejected before, and I didn't know how to deal with that feeling. I couldn't rationally cope like a normal person so I did what anyone else would've done, hit up a bar and sleep with the first person who batted his eyes at me. It wasn't one of my best moments.

I still remembered the disgusting stench of his drunk breath as he forced me to do all the work, just to leave right after. I felt like such a prostitute, except I didn't get paid. You would think my destructive cycle would've ended after that experience, but it only spiraled even more out of control, and soon, I found myself dating a new guy every month.

I had become obsessed with dating apps, finding it all too easy to swipe through hundreds of potential suitors in a single night.

And that's when I met Bill Morelli, a young and handsome Italian musician who lived at the gym and loved getting high. He had blond hair, beautiful blue eyes, and a sexy jawline. He was as stunning as a god, and I knew I loved him at first sight. However, even before we met up, I had set myself up for disaster.

Despite him explicitly telling me that he didn't want a relationship with anyone, and that he only joined the app to fool around with different girls, I met up with him anyway, thinking to myself that I could convince him to love me.

It was summertime, and we met up at an outdoor bar by the pier. I wore a short summer dress that matched the brown highlights I had gotten when I moved to LA, hoping I could snag him with just my outfit alone. I arrived early and texted him my location after I bought a beer and sat down.

"Hey, beautiful." I heard above me minutes later.

The bright sun was blinding my eyes, but I was still able to make out the beautiful jawline I found myself dreaming about.

"Hey, you made it! I was a little worried you'd bail," I joked, my chuckle giving away my awkwardness.

"Nah, I could never pass up the chance to meet someone as gorgeous as you. Hey! Beer!" he exclaimed as he pointed to my drink. "I need one of those. Where do I get one?"

I pointed towards the bar stand a couple feet to the right, and he skipped right over. As he waited in line to order, I couldn't help but wonder whether I was making the right decision. He was definitely cute, not as cute as his pictures, but still cute enough to steal my heart.

"So, what'd you get?" I asked when he sat back down.

"A summer shandy. It's my *favorite* summer drink. So refreshing!" he said enthusiastically.

His energy was contagious. I was so used to being alone and sulking in my own misery that his optimism was strange to me. Even when I hung around Avery, our negative demeanor towards the world was usually on the same level. With Bill, I was left wondering how someone could be so happy and enthusiastic in a world that chewed you up alive and spat you out.

"So, Aria, how come you're single?" Bill asked with an adorable smirk. "If I was looking for a serious relationship, I'd scoop you up immediately."

I cringed at his question. How was I supposed to answer that? How was I supposed to just sit there in front of this god and tell him that I wanted a relationship with him? Even the thought of him sleeping with other girls made me fill up with envy.

"I don't know. Shitty luck, I guess. Every time I find someone I get along with, they leave. I'm just bad luck. What about you? Why are you single?" I asked.

"Heh," he laughed nervously. "To be honest, I'm not. I have a girlfriend, a fiancé, actually, but I like meeting new people. I believe in love and all that, but I just don't think I'm fully ready to settle down yet, you know? My wedding is coming up in a few months, and my nerves are just skyrocketing. I feel like I haven't gotten the chance to expand my horizons enough to never get that chance again."

"So…why did you get engaged if you're not ready to commit to one person?" I should've seen his relationship as a red flag, but I couldn't stop staring at his delicious lips, and all I wanted to do was kiss him.

"I don't know, just two young kids who thought they belonged together, I guess," he mumbled. "Hey! I know a hookah bar right around the corner. You in? You'll love it, I swear!"

Shrugging my shoulders, I stood up and followed him. What did I really have to lose anyway? My life already sucked; who cares if I got high? But his words did make me think of Avery. Maybe we *were* just two kids in young love, stupidly filled with infatuation, and we didn't really love each other as much as we thought.

Maybe all these years of being hung up on him, it was all just an innocent crush. I was also not in the mood to date someone who was already in an intimate relationship, but I couldn't find the courage to leave. I just wanted to taste him so bad.

I spent most of the night stuck in my own head, chuckling to Bill's terrible jokes here and there as we smoked. I never tried hookah before, and I hated everything about it, from the way it smelled to the way it tasted. But apparently, it was one of Bill's favorite activities, so I went along with it, hoping he'd like me more if I did. I wanted to be the cool girl, the girl he'd want to hang out with.

I didn't know what I was thinking by still being around him. Maybe I low-key hoped that he'd break up with his fiancé for me. Or maybe I was so alone that I craved human companionship so much that it didn't matter who I was with.

"The night's still young. I'm staying in a hotel downtown. Wanna pop over for a drink or two?" he asked when the owner of the bar told us they were closing and kicked us out.

"You trying to kidnap me or something?" I joked, hoping he'd find my sense of humor charming.

"Maybe, just maybe," he winked at me.

I decided to go with him. I was living all alone and had no obligations to be home. Plus, I didn't put on my sexiest bra and underwear for nothing. I knew following him to his hotel room meant we were going to have sex, and in that moment, that was all I wanted.

"Welcome to my casa!" Bill shouted when we walked in.

It was a nice hotel, even for LA standards. I had never been in a place so luxurious and regal before that I immediately took my heels off and plopped myself onto the couch.

"This is sick!" I said, excited. "Do you live here?"

"It's like my second home," he nodded as he poured out two glasses of wine. "I'm originally from San Diego, but I come here often as I have a lot of business trips in LA."

"Speaking of business trips, you never told me what you do," I said, accepting one of the glasses from him. "Merlot, my favorite."

"I'm a consultant, for pharmaceutical companies. Most of the big names are in LA. I don't mind it here, except for the smell," he laughed.

"Haha, yeah, I moved here about five years ago, and it still bothers me." By this point, after several beers, the hookah, and now the wine, I felt myself feeling tipsy and lightheaded. "Hey, Bill, I like you. I don't care that you have a fiancé. I really, really like you."

Bill Morelli smiled as he sipped his wine. "I'm so glad you said that. I like you too! You're so beautiful and sexy. All night, all I wanted to do was rip off that dress of yours."

Bill leaned over slowly, brushed my hair behind my ear, and gently kissed my upper lip. I kissed him back, and within seconds, we were engulfed in a kiss of unconditional passion. His hands wrapped around my waist and traveled lower and lower until I found one riding up the skirt of my dress. He lifted his t-shirt over his head, and all I could do was drool over his delicious abs as I leaned down to lick them.

After tossing his shirt onto the floor, he unbuckled his jeans and threw his belt out of sight before leaning over me and unzipping my dress. I stood up and could feel my dress falling off, exposing the transparent lingerie set I was wearing underneath.

"Wow," he whispered when he looked at me. "You're sexier than I imagined."

"And it's all for you," I smiled as I climbed on top of him, my breasts almost popping out of my bra as he embraced me and kissed my neck and chest.

I continued to move my hips over his pelvic area as I felt him rising beneath me. When I planted another kiss on his lips, he loosened my bra straps and completely unwrapped the top half of my body. I had been intimate on first dates before, but this experience sent me over the edge as I found myself falling hard for him. I moaned when he lowered his head and placed soft kisses on my right breast before moving to my left.

Then he flipped me over and laid me down on my back, kissing my body as I twisted and twirled my fingers in his hair, pulling him closer to me. He pulled off the last thing I had remaining on my body and stripped himself down to nothing, penetrating me and letting our physical desires speak for themselves.

Our breaths became more and more heavy, moan after moan escaping my lips as he continued to thrust his naked body against mine. It didn't take long before Bill became more intense, moving faster and faster, until one last moan left my lips, and both our bodies turned limp.

"How long has it been since you last had sex? Not that I'm complaining, but you were pretty tight," Bill panted as he pulled himself off me and fell over to the side, one hand still cupping my bare breast while the other explored between my legs.

"Geez, I don't even know. It's been a while. I really needed this," I responded in embarrassment, kissing him on the lips once again.

"You and me both."

He gave me another affectionate smile and began to move his head down towards my legs. I wasn't sure what he was up to until I found him spreading me open and inserting his tongue inside me. I let the feeling of ecstasy take over, my eyes heavy, my body relaxed. I had the hottest guy in the world going down on me, and I couldn't ask for anything better.

***

The chirping of the birds and the rays of the sun woke me up the next morning. I found myself on the floor of Bill's hotel room with him sleeping next to me, both of us still naked. I stumbled over to my purse and pulled out an aspirin. This wasn't my first rendezvous; I learned the hard way that I had to always be prepared.

"Shit, I'm late for work," I panicked when I looked at the time on my phone.

After getting dressed, I walked out the door without saying a word and called a cab. I was sure I wouldn't hear from Bill again. He was engaged. Of course, he wouldn't want anything more from me than one night of fun. However, when I got home, my phone rang with a call from an unknown number.

"Hey, Aria. Why'd you leave? I rolled over this morning thinking I could play with you a bit more, but you were gone," Bill asked on the other line.

Bill? I didn't think I'd ever hear from him again, but I was glad I did. I felt close to him, a sexual connection, and I wanted to explore his body more.

"Sorry, I was late for work. I had a great time last night," I answered, my cheeks turning red.

"Me too! I would love to get together again. You're so amazingly beautiful, and I really want to hang out again. Are you free tonight?" he asked cheerfully.

"Uh…sure. Let me text you my address. You can come over any time after 8."

My face felt flustered. I couldn't believe this was happening. I was so excited to see his charming face again that I could barely hold my excitement together.

"Perfect! I'll be there!" he chimed before hanging up.

I could feel him smiling on the other side, and it made my heart melt. I wanted him so much.

***

When Bill knocked on my door later that night, I surprised him by wearing a satin robe with absolutely nothing beneath it. His smile stretched wide on his face when he saw me, and he was carrying a bottle of whiskey. I could smell his fragrant cologne from beneath his leather jacket and saw the excitement in his pants.

"Hi! Come on in," I ushered him inside before quickly closing the door.

"Thanks, you have a beautiful apartment! So colorful and southwestern. I dig it. Oh, I almost forgot! I have a surprise for you," he said joyfully as he took a brown paper bag out from his pocket. "My friend brought these *amazing* shrooms all the way back from South America. I hear they give you a trip like you're floating in outer space. I figured we could both try some together."

I never got high before I met Bill, his charm so infatuating that I found myself doing things that were completely out of my comfort zone. But I didn't want to be a party pooper and tell him no. I didn't want him to leave because he didn't think I was cool enough to hang out with. So, I took one out from the bag and popped it in my mouth. I instantly felt my mind spiraling out of control, seeing five different versions of Bill, and they were all in different dimensions. Bill then popped a couple into his mouth as well.

Before I knew what I was doing, I leaned over to Bill and confessed my love for him. I told him everything, from how I wanted a serious relationship with him to how I wanted him to break up with his fiancé and date me instead to how sexy I thought his naked body was. But it didn't seem like he was sober enough to understand me. Instead, he simply brushed my words aside, took off his jacket, and said, "Let's have some fun."

He got up from his chair, lifted me up as he stood over me, and untied my robe, letting it fall to the floor as he admired my nude presence. He moved closer and kissed me, his tongue curious and adventurous. He then picked me up and carried me in his arms to my bed, laying me down. I could tell he was hungry, hungry for me, and I loved it.

My body lusted over the idea of having Bill inside me again as his hands slid across my skin. Pulling out a condom, he slipped it on before slipping inside me, moaning and thrusting with sensual passion, my blood coursing through my veins as he explored me with his hands and tongue.

However, our party was interrupted by the sound of his phone. Bill picked it up while still inside me but quickly pulled out when he looked at who was on the screen.

"Babe, sweetheart, Aria, your body is so beautiful, and I just want to take all of you for myself, but I have to go. Raincheck on that orgasm?" He quickly pulled his shirt over his head and slipped on his shoes before bolting out the door.

Son of a bitch. I bet it's that damn fiancé of his. She doesn't deserve him. I thought to myself as I pulled my robe back on before pouring out a glass of wine. All of a sudden, Avery popped into my thoughts.

"Why did you leave, Avery? Why didn't you answer your phone that night? Why didn't you choose me?" I whispered to myself in the empty apartment. "Why did you choose Jessica over me? She doesn't deserve you. You don't even love her. Why did you make me suffer, put me through all that hell of wanting you when you chose someone else instead? I called you, over and over, and each time, you just sent me to voicemail. I love you, Avery. I hate you for not wanting me."

By this point, tears were streaming heavily from my eyes, and I was hugging my body close to myself. I literally felt my heart breaking as I continued to reminisce over my closest and oldest friend, crying and drinking until I passed out on the kitchen floor.

***

I woke up to my alarm blaring the next morning, my head throbbing with so much pain that I couldn't tell whether it was from all the wine or the shrooms. It was 10am, and I was in no shape to go to work. Besides, I had enough vacation days saved up to take half a year off. Instead, I popped in several aspirins, climbed in the shower, and rang Bill.

"Hello?" he answered.

"Hey, handsome, when can I see you again?" I asked in my most seductive voice.

"Yes…yes, Mr. Nikham. I'll have that paperwork on your desk first thing tomorrow morning," he responded. I knew that was key that his fiancé was there with him. What the hell was she doing there anyway? "Hey, Aria, sorry, I had to step out. Kayla flew here for a surprise visit."

My envy pumped with rage as I tried to remain calm. I wanted Bill all to myself, and the fact that he was still with that bitch made me want to scream. "Wanna come over tonight? I still have those shrooms that you left here."

"Sounds like fun," he said in a deep voice. "I have to drive Kayla to the airport tonight, but I can be over there by 11. Sound good?"

"Absolutely perfect," I answered with an evil smile.

After we hung up, I knew I had to do something to get rid of Kayla. I hated her guts, and as long as Bill and I were together, he couldn't have anyone else in his life. If

Kayla knew her fiancé was cheating on her, she'd definitely call off their engagement and relationship. Bill had told me once that Kayla preferred monogamous relationships, but he didn't like being tied down so he explored other options behind her back. If he were to be exposed, she'd surely dump him.

So, break them up I did. I bought a disposable phone with a random number and sent Kayla all the photos and texts that Bill had sent me over the past few days, minus my name, of course. Luckily, during our last sexual adventure, I pulled her number from his unlocked phone without him knowing.

It didn't take long before I received a call from Bill telling me that his fiancé had left him and asking if he could come over to use me as a distraction. Innocently, I agreed and pretended to not know anything. I thought I was so cunning. I thought I had Bill's heart at the palm of my hand, not realizing that it would all come back to bite me in the ass.

When Bill arrived later that night, I had aromatic candles already lit in the bedroom with a set of silk sheets I had bought earlier that day. I wanted things to be perfect when Bill asked me to be his girlfriend. I was so sure that would happen. Instead, all he wanted was a night of sex with minimal conversation. He said he wasn't ready for another relationship yet and just wanted someone he could fool around with. I agreed, to my demise, hoping he would come around eventually after seeing how much I could give him.

I took him by the hand and led him to the bedroom, where I stripped down to absolutely nothing. I saw his eyes widen before he also stripped down to nothing and pushed me against the wall, kissing me hard and grinding his hips against me in a rush of passion and fire.

***

Weeks turned into months, and as time passed, this became our new routine. We'd always begin our nights by getting high, either on shrooms or with a joint, and then we'd get intimate, on a bed, the couch, inside his car, sometimes in a public alley, wherever. It was a limitless cycle of sexual adventure that I didn't want to end.

Whenever one of us felt bored or alone, we'd call the other and meet up. Bill became, not only my need for satisfaction, but my addiction. He became this physical object that allowed me to forget about reality and all my problems.

Chapter Eleven

After Jessica and I broke up, I fell into a deep hole of self-pity and self-blame. I knew it was my fault that she cheated on me. I had been so focused on chasing Aria and making her mine that I had forgotten about what was already mine. I made Jess a lot of false and empty promises that I never intended to keep, all just to keep myself from feeling lonely.

As time passed, I started to grow more and more angry, my mind turning into my own worst enemy. One night, I fell asleep while sipping my eighth glass of whiskey. I dreamt about Aria coming into my apartment, looking as beautiful as ever, as I was taking a call from a potential client.

"Honey, Avery, it's time for bed. It's lonely all by myself. Come, join me," Aria said to me as she leaned over me and gave me a hug.

"Just give me a sec. I need to make one more call," I answered lazily, my body melting in her arms as she held me.

"No, come on, you need to get some rest. I'll give you a relaxing massage. I know how much you love those," Aria took my phone and turned it off before giving me a kiss on the cheek.

"Wait, I was in the middle…" I began to mumble but was interrupted by her lips on top of mine as her tongue danced with mine in a passionate kiss.

All of a sudden, Jovial walked into the room, and Aria quickly pecked me on the cheek before walking over and jumping onto him, her legs wrapped around him as they made out right in front of me.

"Aria, what the hell is this? Why are you kissing this tool?" I asked. "We're supposed to be together."

"Oh, Avery, naïve Avery, you know I can never settle for just one guy. I need to explore my options. See what else is out there for me."

She blew me a kiss before kissing Jovial one more time, and I stared in betrayal as the two of them walked off together.

I woke up from my nightmare in sweat and loud screams, but luckily for me, there was no one around to hear me. I grabbed my glass off the table and took one last sip before smashing it into pieces against the floor. I didn't care about the mess I had just made. I didn't care about the $50 glass I had just destroyed. Frankly, I didn't care about anything anymore.

Whiskey had become part of my daily routine of self-loathing, and I would find comfort in it every night. The whiskey made room for gin, the gin made room for vodka, and soon, I found myself drowning and on the way to becoming an alcoholic. The worst part was, I didn't give a fuck about any of it.

***

One night, I finally decided to break out of my destructive habit, by heading out to a strip club. I hadn't been with anyone after Jess, and my body was beginning to feel deprived, missing the touch of another human body.

"I just need a distraction, a worry-free night to take my mind off my problems," I said to myself as I flipped through pictures of Aria and the sketches I made of her.

I'd never been to a strip club before, my curiosity getting the best of me. But through Internet searches and forums on how to deal with loneliness, strip clubs popped up the most often, so I thought I'd give it a shot.

Who knows? Maybe I'll end up finding someone nice, someone I can call my next partner.

When I first walked in, I was overwhelmed by the loud music and neon lights. People were grinding on each other on the dance floor, and the place smelled so foul I thought I was going to faint. The room was dimly lit, and there were velvet couches scattered throughout, with crowds of people smoking from large vapes.

The smell of weed was potent in the air, and I could see other illegal drugs being passed around. Strippers were walking around in thin lingerie left and right, a few even fully nude. Some of them were sitting on top of men, young and old, their chests close to their faces;

others were so lost to the drugs that they seemed genuinely disoriented and confused.

There were so many different sounds around me that I didn't know what to focus my ears on; girls were giggling, guys were moaning, and all over, the music blasted so loud through the speaker that I could feel my internal organs beating and thumping. My heart was racing, not sure how to act in the situation, and to be honest, I was a little scared of the unfamiliar environment.

"Hey, handsome. You looking for someone, or just a little fun?" One of the strippers approached me and asked, placing her hand on top of mind.

She was wearing a transparent corset that left too little for the imagination. She had the face of traditional beauty, large eyes, a symmetrical jawline, and hair so smooth and pure that anyone, men and women alike, would be envious of.

"I'm Liana. What brings a young, sexy man like you to a place like this? I'm surprised your girlfriend doesn't have you staying at home," she added as she sat down close to me.

"Uh…I don't have a girlfriend. I'm here alone. I just need a distraction," I said nervously, unsure of what to even say in situations like this. "Hey, where's the bar? I can really go for a whiskey."

"Distraction, you say? I think I have *just* the thing for you." She grabbed my hand and led me to the back. "Follow me," she said with a wink.

When we got to the back room, it was very old and looked like a brothel. There was a small bed in the middle with a huge mirror in front. There was also barely room for anything else, and I immediately knew where this was headed.

"Whiskey for the sexy lad?" Liana said temptingly as she poured some into a glass and handed it to me.

Running on withdraw, I quickly grabbed the glass from her and chugged to my heart's content before asking for more. As I drank, she leaned down and began to unbuckle my belt.

"Wait, I can't...I don't think I can do this," I said quietly.

I knew I sounded pathetic when those words exited my mouth. Why was I even there if I didn't want sex? But I felt guilty for cheating on Aria, even though we weren't together. It was different when it was with Jess. She was my babe, and Aria knew about us. There's just something about sleeping with a stripper that made me feel so...so dirty.

"Oh, don't be shy. It's the reason you're here, right?" Liana smiled and continued to undress me.

By this point, I had drunk so much whiskey that I couldn't even think straight. All I could do was lie back and enjoy the moment. Jess was the only girl I had ever slept with, and it felt strange to feel pleasure from someone else. Good, but strange.

"I miss you, Aria," I whispered before letting my body fall victim to the roaming hands of Liana.

When I woke up hours later, I found myself still in the room, sleeping beside the naked woman passed out next to me, stripped down to nothing. I couldn't remember anything that had happened. I was in such a daze that I couldn't recollect anything from the night before other than how amazing and stress-free I had felt.

I wanted to keep the moment alive for as long as I could. I continued seeing Liana every night, sometimes even chatting about the stressors in our own lives before jumping into bed. We became really close, and I began to see her as more of a companion than just a warm body.

***

A year later, I asked her to marry me.

***

"Sir?" I looked up from scrolling through my phone when Kimiko walked in and interrupted me. "Just a little reminder, you have a business meeting tomorrow in Los Angeles. I have your plane ticket and schedule all ready to go."

"Alright, thanks," I replied. "Just put them next to my briefcase."

I pulled up Aria's message again.

Aria: Hey, Avery. I miss you. Grab a drink with me soon?

Why now, Aria? Of all the times you could've texted me, why now?

Chapter Twelve

Aria's Story
Friends Reconnected

It was a warm summer afternoon when I went to find Bill in his hotel room, another day of smoking pot and hooking up. We had been seeing each other for a while now, and it was his turn to get the party started that night.

However, as soon as I entered the lobby, I saw a familiar face near the elevator, a face I never thought I'd see again.

Avery? I thought. *What the hell was he doing here? And why didn't he ever text me back*

I texted him two weeks ago when I went home to visit my family, and all I got was radio silence. I knew he was living in New York, and my parents were only two hours from him. His face was plastered all over the media as "the fresh face of Wall Street." I could've really used that drink, but I figured he still hated me and wanted nothing to do with me.

Besides, I was sure he and Jess were married by now. They were always so close.

I automatically opened my mouth to call his name, but stopped myself at the last minute. I was sure he didn't know I lived in LA, and I sure as hell couldn't have him finding out that I was there to meet up with some guy. Still, I found myself curious to see what he was up to, but now was not the time. Bill was waiting, and I could only deal with so many guys at a time.

I couldn't risk having Avery see me, so I ducked behind a large pot and bolted down the escalator, texting Bill to have him come over to my place instead.

Bill: Sure, be there in twenty.

When Bill finally arrived at my apartment, he had a bouquet of flowers in his hand.

"I'm feeling some margaritas today. What do you say?" I suggested when he walked in.

"Sure, why not? Anything you want," Bill replied with a smile.

We quickly jumped into bed after about four glasses each, tearing off each other's clothes while we were both disoriented. Sex was rushed but passionate, and I was shaking with pleasure.

However, as we were both nearing the finish line, I inadvertently screamed out Avery's name. I knew that even though Bill and I agreed that this relationship wasn't serious, he was still hurt by what I had said.

No one wants to hear the other person moan someone else's name while having sex.

He didn't even finish before pulling out and quickly throwing on his clothes. He was out the door before I had a chance to say anything else. I knew I fucked up, drinking the rest of the tequila before sending him an apology text and passing out on the couch.

***

The next morning, I expected Bill to respond to my message, but all I saw was a read notification. I thought it was strange. He was usually so eager to text me back, always excited to talk to me, but now, he had suddenly changed. I knew it was because of my slip-up in calling him "Avery," but I didn't think I'd find what I discovered next.

After growing infuriated by his lack of response, I decided to visit his hotel room in hopes of apologizing to him in person instead. I thought that maybe he was expecting me to say sorry to his face instead of copping out through a text message.

However, when I arrived and entered his room using a spare key card he had given me, I found him fucking another girl. Not Kayla, but someone new completely.

"Who the hell is this?" I shouted as I barged in.

Bill and the girl, a girl of perfect stature with her long blonde hair and petite slim body, jumped in surprise, the girl pulling the sheets over her naked body as Bill just stared at me, his face apathetic.

"Why didn't you answer any of my calls? And who the fuck is she?" I screamed again.

"Excuse me, Mare. I'll be just one sec," Bill turned to the girl before grabbing my wrist and pulling me into the bathroom. He was still completely nude, and all I could focus on was his dangling package.

"What the hell, dude? You ignore all my messages just for me to find you with some slut? Who is she anyway?" I demanded, my voice raising.

"That, is my girlfriend, Mare," Bill replied without hesitation. "You were totally hung up on someone else, so I decided to move on and find someone new. Besides, I was getting bored of you anyway. All you ever want to do is drink, and you're never interested in being adventurous in bed."

I stared in shock. I was having such a great time fooling around with Bill that I never thought it would end so soon, so suddenly. "Can we still see each other? I can be more experimental," I pleaded with sorry eyes, but he couldn't even look at me.

"Aria, you were a great distraction, but you have to move on. We're done here. I'm seeing someone else now. Please, just go," he sighed before gesturing me out the room and closing it behind me.

I could hear the sound of the bed rustling on the other side. How could he have used me and dumped me so quickly? I gave him everything, and he just treated me like a piece of meat. Though, as it may be, I wasn't surprised. I had a history with men who would only use me and then dump me for someone better. Just my luck.

Of all the men in my life, Avery was the only one who ever treated me with some kind of respect. Even Xander would glare at other girls when I wasn't looking or would flirt with them right in front of me.

***

Over the next few weeks, I tried my best to avoid negative thoughts while my drug habits increased. I always thought it was Bill's influence that drove me to these behaviors, but it was me all along. Who would've guessed?

One night, during one of my solo bar-hopping excursions, I found myself standing in front of Bill's hotel, half-drunk, and still very livid.

"Fuck you! Fuck you and all your fucking LIES!" I screamed as I threw my beer bottle against the wall, the bottle shattering into pieces. I was about to leave, but suddenly, a familiar face walked out of the building.

"Aria?" The face asked, "Is that you?"

"Aria? I'm not Aria. My name is Princess Contessa, ruler of the Planet Nebula!" I shouted. I didn't know what I was thinking, or who was speaking to me, but I had drunk way too much to notice or care. From what I could see at that moment, I was speaking to a little purple gremlin.

"Are you okay?" the gremlin asked. "You don't look so good."

"Aww, it speaks!" I cheered as I jumped up and down. "The little gremlin speaks!"

"Aria, knock it off! It's me, Avery. Remember? You're hallucinating," the gremlin continued to defend himself as he spoke to me in a squeaky voice.

"You're not Avery. I know Avery. Avery isn't purple, and he certainly doesn't have a beard," I chuckled as I fell over.

Luckily, the gremlin caught me just in time to prevent me from scratching up my face. "But you definitely feel like Avery. Those biceps are really treating you well," I continued, stroking his thick arms.

"Alright, let's get you inside before you start making out with the sidewalk." Before I knew it, he picked me up and carried me into the hotel, my eyes closing in slumber from the intoxication.

***

When I woke up the next morning, I found myself in what I assumed was one of Avery's t-shirts.

Did he undress me last night?

I had such a pounding headache that I didn't know what was going on. I looked over to my right and saw Avery sleeping soundly next to me, shirtless. I had no idea what was happening, but I wasn't exactly complaining. His arm was draped over me, and I struggled to remember whether we did anything last night.

Is this a dream? Am I still hallucinating? I was pretty tripped up last night; anything could've happened.

I pinched myself hard before pinching Avery on the shoulder, just hard enough to wake him up but not enough to actually hurt him. I had to know whether this was real.

"Huh?" Avery murmured beside me, waking up, and rubbing his eyes. "You up?"

"Morning…" I managed to say, not sure what time it actually was.

"Good morning," Avery sat up next to me, looking at me with concerned eyes. "How are you feeling? Need anything for that hangover?"

Avery smiled while tucking my hair behind my ear. He got up, not waiting for an answer, and returned seconds later with some toast and a glass of orange juice.

"Um, thanks… What are you doing in LA? I didn't think I'd see you again," I asked.

"Just business stuff. I own a company back in New York, and there was a partner meeting here yesterday. Thought I'd stay for a couple extra days since I did fly all the way here. You know, explore the city a bit. I've never been here before," Avery replied, staring at me the same way he did when we were young.

"Oh, cool. I'd love to hear more about your business one day. I feel like we have a lot of catching up to do! Hey, where are my clothes…? And why am I wearing your shirt?" I asked, half-joking, but also very serious.

"Don't worry, nothing happened," he assured me. "You puked all over yourself and my sheets which, by the way, I'm billing you for, so I had to get you changed so you wouldn't get sick. I tried to wake you up, but man, you were really out of it. Also, did you know you snore like a bulldozer?"

"Stop it! No, I don't," I shouted playfully as I gave him a friendly punch on the arm.

I wanted to ask him why he never texted me back. I wanted to find out why he never called me all those years, but I didn't want to ruin what we had going at the moment. I didn't want to do anything that would put him in an uncomfortable position.

Avery ordered room service while my clothes were sent to the laundromat, and we ate breakfast in bed together, just like the good old days when we were kids. It brought back many wonderful memories that I wanted to cherish forever.

"Hey, Aria, I have a pretty packed day today, but I'm in LA for a couple more days. Can we meet up again? I feel like we have some catching up to do," he stammered before taking another bite of his pancakes.

Nervous, I pushed myself to agree. I had already lost him once, and I wasn't going to let that happen again, even if my nerves refused to stop fighting me on it.

Chapter Thirteen

Avery's Story
Feelings Returned

I never thought I'd see Aria ever again. After the last time she rejected me, I swore her off for good, refusing to pick up her calls or answer her texts. Not like it was difficult for me anyway; she didn't exactly reach out to me after the night of the party, until a couple weeks ago.

It was so strange seeing her again, so strange, but also a disaster. I had spent years forgetting about her, pushing thoughts of her away from my mind. Now, after seeing her again, all those memories and feelings came rushing back, all that hard work, gone.

***

Two days later, I invited myself over to Aria's. She was a little hesitant, but I guilt-tripped her into letting me come. We both had a lot of explaining to do, and I had to head back home soon, so it was now or never. However, I was nervous about potentially meeting her boyfriend. I wasn't sure if she was with Xander or Jovial or whatever other man she decided to pick up off the streets.

I rang the bell, and all I could hear on the other side was, "Shit, shit, shit," before the sound of glass shattering.

"Hi!" Aria said with an uncomfortable grin when she finally opened the door. "You're here early."

I just stared at her. I was only five minutes early and already suspected that she had a guy somewhere in her apartment that she hadn't gotten the chance to mosey out yet. "Um, not really? Can I come in?"

"Yeah, yeah, yeah. Come on in," she said in a rush as she gestured me in. "Just give me like two minutes. I'll be right back. Do you want anything while I'm gone? Coffee? Water? Breakfast?"

"Breakfast? It's three in the afternoon," I responded in confusion.

"Right… Be right back!"

About a minute after she pranced away, I could hear the sound of rustling and whispering near the kitchen. Either she had become mentally insane, or she was trying to sneak someone out. I knew I wasn't her boyfriend or anything, but damn, did she really have to cut her sex sessions so close?

"Where's your boyfriend?" I asked humorously when she walked back into the living room with two cups of coffee.

"What? Oh, no, I don't have a boyfriend," she replied nonchalantly as if nothing had happened.

I wanted to pry more, to see what the hell she was up to, but she clearly didn't want to talk about it, and I didn't want to drive her away again.

"Really? What happened to Jovial? Weren't you two living together?"

"No, and it just didn't work out. He wasn't really my type anyway. Too arrogant for my taste," she answered as she took a sip from her cup.

And that's how it started. We continued catching up on all the years we missed out on in each other's lives, just two friends chatting about life like we did when we were kids. How I missed hearing her playful laugh and sweet voice. She was the same Aria I remembered.

Soon, the sun turned to the moon, and daylight turned to night. I didn't realize how long we'd been talking until she dozed off on the couch. Holy crap, it's midnight. I took her in my arms, gave her a long hug, and brought her to bed before tucking her in. I then placed a soft kiss on her forehead and let myself out.

"I love you, Aria," I whispered to myself as I closed the door.

***

Early morning the next day, I called Aria as soon as I woke up, hoping she'd answer my call. I had such a great time hanging out with her that I found myself wanting to be around her all the time.

"Good morning, sunshine!" I said cheerfully.

"Avery? Are you insane? It's six in the morning…" Aria murmured, still half asleep. "What do you want?"

"I wanted to see if you'd like to go shopping today. I need to pick up a few things, and since you're a regular Angelino now, I was wondering if you'd be interested in showing me around."

"And you couldn't have waited until later to ask?" she asked, her voice sounding annoyed.

"Nope!" I knew Aria. And I knew she found joy in my playful teasing. Pestering her like I didn't care was one of my sure-fire ways to get her to do what I wanted.

"Fine," she reluctantly agreed, and I cheered silently on the other end.

"Alright, see you then! Oops, gotta go. Someone's calling. Bye!"

I hung up my call and saw Liana on the other line. Fuck. What the hell was I going to tell my wife? She knew about Aria, and she also knew that I used to love her. If she found out that Aria was also in LA, she's going to suspect something and flip out.

"Hey, honey," I said as I picked up.

"Hey, babe, how's LA? How'd the business meeting go?" she asked on the other line.

"It was great! They signed on as a new partner. This is going to be great for my business."

"Congrats! I'm so happy for you! By the way, Loria and Cooper say hi. They miss their daddy. When are you coming home?"

"In a few more days. I want to make sure I really close with them to avoid taking any chances. Hey, can I call you back tonight? I have to run to a meeting."

"Sure, Avery, I love you," Liana said quietly.

"I love you too," I whispered.

What have I done? I thought to myself as I hung up the phone.

I got so hung up on seeing Aria again that I completely forgot that I was still married. I couldn't hurt Liana like this. She always supported me, even when I struggled to get my business started and had nothing. But

Aria, sweet, beautiful Aria. Aria meant everything to me, and she was the love of my life.

But Liana. But Aria. I was so conflicted between the two women in my life, just like I had been when I was with Jess.

Noon soon struck, and I pushed aside my thoughts to pick up Aria. She was wearing a black dress with white sneakers, cute as a button, her hair perfectly curled, and her lips a bright shade of red. She was absolutely stunning.

"Damn, you really cleaned yourself up. The first time I saw you in LA, you were a hot mess," I winked.

"Thanks, but I'm a slob most of the time, as I'm sure you remember from me rubbing spaghetti sauce all over myself as a kid," she joked and smiled at me, enough to melt my heart again. "What do you need to pick up anyway?"

"A gift for you," I grinned.

"No, seriously, what do you need?" she asked again.

"Mmm, I think I'm feeling some ice cream. Maybe a root beer float," I joked again, trying to get a rise out of her.

"That's…that's not what I expected to hear, but let's just go. There's a really delicious place inside the mall on Sunset. We should go there." She sounded frustrated, but I could see her trying to hide her smile. I knew I was in.

As I drove, Aria pointed out different places along the way that she'd been to, mostly bars and restaurants, but that's what I loved about her. Her eclectic taste. Twenty minutes later, we arrived at Park Place, a mall in the city known for its fashion, luxury, and arts. We both ordered root beer floats, our favorite since we were kids.

I thought back to how we used to spend every weekend during the summer finding places that served root beer floats, comparing the many different ones to see which was best. Marrie's was always my favorite; Aria could never decide. She just loved to eat.

"What are you looking at?" Aria asked as she caught me staring at her, sipping my float.

"You got a little…" I gestured to her mouth where some whipped cream was sitting. "Here, let me get it for you."

Softly, I ran my thumb across her upper lip, coming really close to her until our faces were about an inch apart. I smiled and licked the cream off my finger. "Delicious!" However, I couldn't stop staring even after I cleaned her off. She smelled so good, and her face was so alluring. I leaned in closer and gave her a kiss.

She didn't stop me until several seconds after she kissed back. "Wait, we can't. You're married."

"I'm sorry, sorry. I couldn't help myself," I apologized quickly as she pulled away.

"We should get going," Aria said.

"Hey, do you want to come back to my place? I have a surprise for you. Don't worry, I won't try anything funny or inappropriate. I think you'll like this."

"Sure," she reluctantly agreed. "But first, I need to buy some hand towels. I've been using mine for the past two years, and they're getting a little gross."

About an hour later, we headed back to the hotel after stopping at a diner for some burgers.

"So, what's the surprise?" Aria asked while putting down her bags.

I pulled out my phone and showed Aria a video call from an anonymous number. I didn't want to ruin it for her, but Jesper and Rosalie were on the other line. They contacted me a few days ago with exciting news.

Honestly, I was surprised they're still together. They were always supportive of each other, but they've had their fair share of on and offs. I even drove down from New York a few years ago to attend their wedding. Aria wasn't invited as she and Rosalie had a falling out about Jess, but since then, Rosalie had wanted to make peace.

"Oh my god! No way! A baby?" she yelled into the screen as soon as they told her the news.

She was just as happy as I was that our two oldest friends were having a baby together. It made me happy knowing that she was happy. It's all I ever wanted.

"Aria, you keep talking. I'll be in the shower," I whispered in her ear before heading into the bathroom. However, I continued to press my ear against the door to eavesdrop as the water ran. I had to know if Aria says anything about me to Rosalie.

"Hey, Aria, I just want to apologize for treating you the way I did when we last spoke. I was not myself. My mom had just passed away, and I was going through a depressive phase. I hope you understand and can forgive me. I think what you have going for you is great!" I heard Rosalie say to Aria.

"It's okay, I get it. I've had my fair share of episodes as well. No hard feelings. I miss being able to talk and hang out with you. We used to be so close. All of us," Aria replied.

"So, how's Steve? Last time I saw you, you were visiting your parents and had him draped around your arm like a scarf. He's super cute. Don't tell Jesper I said that," Rosalie asked.

Steve? Who the hell was Steve? I thought Jovial and Xander were her only serious boyfriends. And now there's Steve? How many more are there? Who's next?

"Oh, that didn't work out. It turned out that we both wanted different things, and he wasn't really ready to commit yet." Aria answered quietly, her voice sounding disappointed that she was still single.

"I'm sure you'll find someone great one day. Keep your head up. I believe in you! Oops, I gotta go. Jesper's waiting for me in the car. Ultrasound appointment. Talk to you soon?" Rosalie said.

"Sure thing," Aria responded before hanging up.

I jumped into the shower quickly while Aria said her goodbyes, and when I emerged from the bathroom with a towel wrapped around my waist, she was still sitting in the same spot. She looked up at me, a look of surprise on her face.

"What the hell, Avery?" Aria yelled when she looked at me and turned back around, blushing.

"What?" I asked, confused.

"Where the *fuck* are your clothes? Go put something on!" she screamed while still facing away.

"Why? It's not like you've never seen me like this," I teased while putting my arm around her.

She quickly pulled me into a playful hug before pushing me away, "Go, now!"

"Now you're just playing with my heart," I smirked and walked into the bedroom.

Spending time with Aria brought back so many wonderful memories, and I started to lift out of the personal misery I was living in while in New York. Sure, I loved my wife and kids, but they always needed something from me; I always felt the pressure to be responsible around them, never getting the chance to be myself and have fun.

With Aria, every day was a thrilling adventure. We'd make each other laugh and dared each other to do stupid things in public. With Aria, I started to live again, become happier, and I could tell that she seemed happier too, more like the Aria I knew as a kid.

Later that night, after Aria left, I called Liana. I was supposed to fly home the next day, but I just couldn't bear to leave Aria. I had to let Liana know what was going on and end my marriage.

"I'm sorry," I whispered as I hung up the phone.

Never did I think I'd get divorced and leave my kids behind. My parents had been married for over 60 years, and I always thought the first girl I married would be my wife forever. But things had changed. Things were more complicated than that. Liana would get custody of the kids, and I would see them on an irregular basis.

I knew I wasn't thinking clearly when I decided to end things so abruptly. Till death do us part, my ass. I was just too naïve and let a childhood crush ruin my marriage.

Aria: Hey, Avery! Can I come back? I forgot to give you something. A present.

My heart jumped when I saw that text from Aria. It made me forget about my family back home, and all I was excited for was Aria. I texted her back and ran to change into something sexier and more attractive from the sweats I was wearing.

"Hey, babe. Fancy seeing you here," I winked at Aria when I opened the door.

"You know, I think I like the towel better," she smiled.

"I think *you'd* look good in a towel," I smiled back as I unwrapped the box.

"It's my sketchbook. I never forgot about you, Avery. Every day, I'd draw you, just like you'd drawn me, so the memory of you will stay in my head for as long as it can. You mean the world to me, Avery. You were my first and only true friend."

I stayed silent. The gift was so touching. She *had* been thinking about me. She *did* care. All these years, I thought it was a lost cause for us, but now that I found out she never stopped thinking about me, I wanted to see this through to the end.

"I love it. I really do," I said and kissed her on the cheek. "It's the best present ever."

"I'm glad. I thought it was kind of corny at first, like you wouldn't really care," she blushed.

"Are you kidding me? You know I love sentimental gifts. It's so touching. Best gift ever! Let's go get some dinner. I'm starving. I came across an amazing Japanese place when I first got here that I instantly fell in love with. What do you say?" I jumped up from the edge of the couch and announced.

As Aria nodded and went home to get changed, I became more excited. This was going to be our first real date. She didn't know it yet, but a big confession was coming her way with lots of romance. I told her to meet me there since she lived a lot closer than I did. When she arrived, dressed in a beautiful red dress and matching heels, I stood there in awe with a bouquet of red roses.

"You look gorgeous," I smiled and led her to the terrace, where I had organized a private romantic candlelit dinner for the two of us.

"What? How? How did you do this so fast?" she asked, confused.

"I didn't," I answered. "I've been planning this for a couple days now, hoping that everything would fall into place, and it did. Aria…" I grabbed her by the hand. "I never stopped thinking about you. I never stopped loving you. I know I didn't answer your call that night at the party, but please, understand that I couldn't. I was so hurt by all the rejections that I didn't want to feel pain anymore. But I was wrong. I was wrong to think that I could live without you. I can't. I want to be with you, Aria. I love you to the moon and back."

"Avery…" As Aria began to speak, I braced myself for another rejection.

Instead, she leaned in, and I grabbed the back of her head and kissed her passionately on the lips. The sparks that always generated between us fired rapid, and soon, we found our bodies being pressed together.

Aria's hands traveled up to my chest, unbuttoning my shirt with quick fingers, our mouths still locked. She wrapped one leg around me, and I tilted her head back to run my tongue across her collarbone and neck. I wanted every piece of her for myself.

I pulled the straps of her dress down slowly, making sure we were out of sight from the rest of the restaurant. I worked my lips around her body as if I was seeing it for the first time, worshipping every part of her. I wanted to savor every minute of this. Aria was pulling my hair, driving me even crazier, pushing against me every time.

Her hands traveled up and down my back, her teeth biting my upper lip as I moaned quietly into her ear. Our warm bodies intertwined under the starry sky and into an eternal embrace. It was the best night of my life.

Chapter Fourteen

It had been nearly a week since Avery left for Los Angeles, and things were beginning to grow hectic at home. Loria and Cooper never stopped asking about their daddy and when he would come home to play with them, pestering my every time I tried to sit and relax.

When I first had the twins, Avery assured me that it'd be fine if I took an early retirement so I could watch after the kids. He had assured me that his business was successful enough where he could carry our entire financial weight, and I'd never have to work again.

"Are you sure?" I asked while tucking the twins into bed one night.

"Positive. I'm the man of the house now. I know how much you want to be a mom so that's all you need to focus on from now on," he smiled at me before kissing me on the forehead. "I love you, Liana. I want to give you everything you deserve."

Things were fine at first, Avery working his usual 9 to 5 before coming home to play with the kids. I stayed home to watch the kids, day and night, even bringing them with me to go grocery shopping, so we didn't have to waste unnecessary money on daycare.

Part of me missed working, the constant interactions I had with people, but Avery kept insisting that I remain a stay-at-home mom, especially since my most recent job hadn't exactly been the most appropriate. Things were going great…until they weren't.

***

A few years later, Avery began to grow more and more distant, coming home in a bad mood and locking himself in his office until it was time for dinner. Even at the dinner table, he barely made any eye contact or conversation with the rest of the family. I knew his personality suited that of a lone wolf, but it seemed like that had become his only demeanor.

And although Avery never told me what was wrong, always covering up his problems by saying it was an "off day," I knew what was really bothering him. And what was bothering him, was Aria.

When I first met Avery, Aria was all he could talk about, how much he loved her and how much he missed her. Even after we got married, he could never really get her off his mind, bringing up her name whenever he saw an opening in conversations. I asked him about Aria before. I was pregnant with the twins at the time, and my emotions had gotten the best of me.

I was curious whether Avery still had feelings for Aria, and I specifically remembered his exact words:

Liana, nothing will ever come between us, not even Aria. You're my one and only.

Part of me didn't believe him then, the sparkle in his eye giving away his true feelings whenever he said her name, but I chose to ignore my instinct and gave him the benefit of the doubt. That was before I stumbled across her text one day when Avery was in the shower.

Aria: Hey, Avery. I miss you. Grab a drink with me soon?

Fucking Aria, you spent all those years playing with my husband's heart while you slept around, and now, you decide to waltz back into his life?

But as much as I wanted to believe it was just a coincidence, that text was also the start of Avery's emotional decline, and I knew it was because of her.

***

A few days after Avery left for LA, I called his cell to check in on how the business meeting went. The meeting was all he had talked about for months leading up to it, calling it "the biggest potential investor his company ever had." However, when he picked up the phone, he sounded distracted, like he didn't even want to talk to me and was in a rush to hang up. I no longer heard the excitement in his voice whenever he spoke about work, and his "I love you" felt automated and forced.

Ever since Avery left for LA, Loria and Cooper had been counting down the days till he came home, immediately disappointed when they found out they would have to wait even longer than anticipated. All the kids ever wanted was for their father to love them and pay attention to them. He did, at first, always making the effort to keep them happy and entertained, but ever since that text, it's like he had become a whole new different person.

***

And I was right. Not long after that conversation, Avery called me in the middle of the night.

"Hello…? Avery? It's one in the morning here. Why are you calling?" I answered groggily as I tried to keep myself from falling back asleep. "Whatever this is, can it wait until the morning?"

"No, it can't. Liana, I want a divorce. You can keep the condo, the kids, all of it. I'm not coming home," he said in such a rush on the other end, like he had been holding these words in for quite a while now.

"What…what do you mean? We're married. You have children here in Manhattan. You're just going to throw it all away? Just like that? Not even talking about it first?" I was shocked. Avery was never someone who acted impulsively, and hearing those words would've made me collapse onto the ground if I wasn't already sitting on the bed. "It's Aria, isn't it? She messaged you, and now, you're so giddy like a middle schooler that you're willing to sacrifice everything for some childhood crush."

"I'm sorry," was all he could say before hanging up.

I'm sorry? I'm sorry? Married all these years with two kids, and that was all the respect he could give me. I was furious.

I guess nice guys aren't so nice after all when given the opportunity to become assholes.

I'd thought we'd be together forever. I had quit my job without any life savings because I thought Avery would take care of me for the rest of my life, like he had promised. Now, I had no job, no money, and two very needy kids who had been spoiled their entire lives. What was I going to do?

I could easily sell the condo and bank the money, but I wanted nothing to do with Avery after the way he treated me. In fact, I couldn't even find myself in Manhattan for another day without breaking down.

***

The next morning, I packed up all our things and moved in with my parents in Tampa, Florida. I didn't want to accidentally run into Avery in case he ever decided to come home after Aria dumps his ass.

I never heard from Avery again. I even waited by the phone over the next several weeks in case he called and wanted to get back together after realizing his mistake. But when one of our mutual friends sent me a picture of Avery and Aria kissing that he had found on social media, I immediately called a lawyer the next day and filed for divorce. I was done with Avery. For good.

I thought I was done with the business forever, but Avery always held the financial wealth, and now being separated, I knew I couldn't continue living off him. My parents didn't have much, struggling to make ends meet as is, so I had no choice but to strip again.

Stripping was never my dream job. I wanted to be a paralegal ever since I was in high school, and stripping was only supposed to be a side hustle so I could save up enough money for school. But then I met Avery, who convinced me I didn't need a job at all, so I gave up my dream. Now that I needed a steady paycheck again, stripping was all I knew.

Several applications later, I was given a position at a new gentlemen's club in Tampa. It was a small establishment, but I knew it would drive a lot of traffic as there wasn't another one for miles away. Walking back into a club that first day brought back so many memories of Avery, how I instantly felt an attraction towards him when I saw him that first day. Those were the days.

I looked around, seeking out my first customer, and saw a reserved middle-aged man sitting alone at the bar, looking back and forth from the front door to the dance floor.

"Hey, handsome. You looking for someone, or just a little fun?" I smiled as I walked over to him and placed my hand on top of his.

Chapter Fifteen

Aria's Story
Best Friends Forever

When I woke up the next morning, the first thing that hit me was my naked body. The second, the naked body lying next to me, arms wrapped around me, and quiet snores.

"Avery," I whispered to myself. I stared at Avery, and all I wanted to do was kiss him again. Our passionate night at the restaurant turned into an even more passionate night back at his hotel.

All of a sudden, my conscience began to fight against me. What the hell was I doing? Avery's married, and he's my best friend. Did I really just sleep with my best friend?

Oh god, what if I'm just a one-night stand to him?

But he told me he loved me. What if he was lying just to get me in bed? Was he going to toss me away and go back to his family in New York? Was he just like every other guy I'd ever been with?

With confusion clouding my mind, I grabbed my clothes, changed, and darted out of the room before he could wake up. By the time I got home, there were tears in my eyes, tears of pain and distraught. My phone rang, but I ignored it. I hopped into the shower, my mind still reeling with questions.

*****

Later that night, when I was walking home from work, I found Avery sitting on the steps of my building, sleeping.

"Huh? What? I have a knife!" he screamed as I startled him to wake him up.

"Avery, chill. It's me. What are you doing here, and this late at night?" I asked, frustrated to see him. I didn't know what his game was, and I didn't want to find out.

"Oh my god, you're alive!" he cheered, wrapping his arms around me.

"Um…yeah? Why wouldn't I be?" I asked, confused.

"I've been calling you all day! You left this morning without saying a word, and I was worried something had happened to you," he replied, a concerned look plastered on his face.

"Ugh, Avery, I don't have time for this. It's been a very long day, and I just want to relax with a glass of wine," I whined, proceeding to unlock my front door.

"No, we need to talk, now. Why did you leave this morning without saying anything? The doorman said you left in a rush, and I know you don't start work until 10am. What's going on?" He was demanding answers, and I didn't have any good excuses for him other than my true feelings.

"Am I just a one-night stand to you? Did you just fuck me to use me? Or to get revenge for all the times I rejected you?" I blurted out.

"What? Why would you ask that? How could you even think that I'd treat you like just another hookup? You know me better than that," he defended his honor.

"Well, it just feels weird that you're married, with a family, and you're here instead of back home, hooking up with me. How am I supposed to feel? Of course, I'm gonna feel like you're using me. I'm basically your mistress!" Tears streamed uncontrollably from my eyes as I tried to wipe them away with my sleeve.

"Hey, hey, Aria, it's okay," Avery comforted me as he hugged me and brushed my cheeks with his thumbs. "You could never be a one-night stand; I love you too much. I was going to wait to tell you, until it was all finalized, but I left my wife. It's over between us. I did it for you. I want you. You're my family now. I choose you over my marriage, and I'll still see my kids, but right now, all I want is you. You were always the most important person in my life, and you always will be. I left my marriage for you because I know we're meant to be." I stared deeply into her eyes and could tell that she felt the same way, though her eyes a little unfocused.

"I wanted to tell you that night, that night at the party that I loved you," I confessed. "After you kissed me, I broke up with Jovial and tried to call you, but you never picked up. I know I deserved it, all those years of blowing you off finally caught up to me."

"Aw, Aria, I'm so sorry! If I had known you felt that way, I would've never ignored you. I was just so tired of getting hurt, and I thought that if I let myself fall back in, you'll just reject me again." Avery softly kissed my lips. "I love you, Aria, more than you could ever know."

Then, to my surprise, he knelt down on one knee and pulled a tiny box out of his coat pocket. "I've been wanting to give you this ever since I first saw you in LA. Aria Xing, will you do me the honor of being my wife?" Avery proposed.

Cars were honking, and people were screaming at us to get a room, but I didn't care. That moment was so romantic that I immediately said yes. I jumped for joy, and we kissed again, Avery carrying me in his arms as we walked inside.

***

Several months later, our wedding day arrived. June 24th. I always wanted a June wedding. The sun shining, and the birds chirping. It was perfect. Everything was perfect. The wedding venue was a warm, inviting space that offered extraordinary views.

The multi-level mansion extended into five distinctive corridors. Natural details like the stone hearth, marble beams, hand-forged ironwork, and carved granite reflected the natural surroundings, with fresh seasonally-inspired cuisine served that day from the best Mediterranean restaurant in town.

"Are you excited?" Mom asked as I stood in front of the mirror in my wedding gown.

"I think so. I mean, he's my best friend. This is a dream come true, childhood friends turned spouses. I couldn't ask for anything more," I answered, continuing to stare into the mirror. "Then why do I feel so guilty? So bad?"

"Oh, honey," Mom tried to console me. "I understand that you're scared. It's a big decision to make. Although, I never pegged you for someone who would settle down and commit to one person. We're very similar in that way."

"What do you mean?" I turned around to face her, her cheeks noticeably red and ashamed.

"Well, let's just say, your brother may not…exactly be your brother."

"Is that why Dad left?" I asked. I wasn't surprised by what she said. I had known for years now that I was just so different from some of the members of my family.

"We'll talk about it later," Mom responded. "Right now, we need to get ready for your big day."

I wore a beautiful dress with a long train, chiffon sleeves, and a laced corset. The skirt resembled that of a fairytale princess, and I had on a matching veil. My "brother" walked me down the aisle since Dad was no longer in the picture, and I smiled at Avery, who was standing up at the altar. I felt myself sweating and tensing up as I stood there with Avery, staring out into the crowd where our families were cheering us on.

I knew it was always a dream come true for both our families to see us end up together. We were always so close.

"I, Aria Xing, take you, Avery Cheung, to be my husband, in good times and bad, in sickness and in health. I promise to honor and love you until death do us part," I said as my mind suddenly flashed back to all the different men I had been with, each one leaving me just as I started to become attached to them.

"Do you, Avery Cheung, take Aria Xing as your lawfully wedded wife, to have and to hold, from this day forward, for better or for worse, for rich or for poor, in sickness and in health, to love and cherish until death do you part?"

"I do." I heard Avery say as the crowd stood up in a standing ovation.

I felt Avery place a ring on my finger as I placed one on his. Was this really happening? Did I really just get married? Avery kissed me on the lips, the first time as husband and wife, and led me down the aisle to our limo. As we walked, I could swear I saw Bill, Steve, Jovial, and Xander all staring back at me, each one dressed in a tuxedo and holding a single red rose.

When we all sat down for the reception, the feast in front of us was full of delicious and gourmet meals. The table was filled with filet mignon, fresh salmon, lobster and clams, a fresh assortment of fruit, and more wine than I could ever imagine. It was a tradition in the Chinese family to always serve a large feast during weddings. Avery's and my family really went all out.

"So, when's the baby coming?" I asked Rosalie, who was sitting beside me at the table. "Are you excited?"

"In about two months. Totally! I'm so psyched! I always wanted to be a mom," she replied, patting her belly. "I always wanted two little girls. I really hope they're twins. Jesper's super excited too. He's been setting up the house for the past seven months, ever since he found out I was pregnant, baby-proofing literally everything and buying things we don't even need!" she added with a laugh.

"Aw, that's great," I smiled. "I love kids. I hope, someday, Avery and I can have one of our own. My mom was always my role model, and I want to carry on that legacy."

"Hey, girls! Stop gabbing, and come down and dance!" Jesper shouted to us as Avery blew me a kiss.

"Let's do it!" Rosalie cheered in excitement as we walked down to the dance floor. Even at seven months pregnant, she was still the enthusiastic and most energetic one out of all of us. I always admire how positive she remained even in horrible situations.

"Shall we dance?" Avery asked when I arrived in front of him.

"We shall," I smiled, taking his hand.

As we danced as a newlywed couple, I couldn't help but think back to my past relationships. Over the past several years, I never thought I would end up settling for my best friend. Yes, I said settling. I had an inkling that I would struggle to settle down and be with one person monogamously when I became obsessed with online dating. There were just so many options out there that I wanted to be with them all, test them out to see what I like and didn't like. I still felt like I hadn't explored enough to really know what I wanted yet.

But here I was, committed with a ring around my finger. Maybe Mom was right. Maybe this *was* a terrible decision.

After the reception, Avery and I drove to our honeymoon in Sedona, Arizona. We booked the most romantic suite tucked between the mountains, decorated entirely with red roses and edible aphrodisiacs.

"Wow, this place looks amazing," I said as we walked into the room. "You really did all this?"

"Of course," Avery replied. "You're more than worth it. Marrying you is a dream come true, and I want every moment of it to be absolutely PERFECT!"

He lit about thirty candles before closing the door behind us as I sat on the bed, my dress spilling all over it. He put on the first song we ever listened to when we were kids.

"I can't wait to grow old with you," he whispered as he sat down beside me, nibbling on my ear.

At that moment, I couldn't help but feel slightly guilty, guilty for not being able to enjoy the moment because I was thinking about other men.

Bill. How devastating it was that you couldn't be the one.

Steve. I thought you liked me. I really thought you did. You said I was the one, someone you'd been searching for your whole life.

Jovial. You fell in love with me during a time when no one else wanted me. You saved me from a battle with myself and gave me everything I asked for. But it was all a lie. I never wanted you. I just wanted you to want me.

And Xander. You were the reason this whole cycle started. If it wasn't for you, I would've been with Avery from the start. Because of you, I'm now stuck in this cycle of confusion when it comes to men, wanting those I can't have and leaving those I can.

Avery. I thought I was done writing my series of back and forth with you. I thought I had finally given up on pushing you away. I love you, but I think I love myself more. We got married in front of our entire family, and now, I feel pressured to stay loyal to you forever. I don't know if I can. You treat me like I'm your princess when I clearly don't deserve it, and I feel like I may struggle to not turn against you if given the chance.

"What's wrong, honey?" Avery stopped and asked as he noticed me distracted by my thoughts.

"I'm sorry. It just feels a little stuffy in here. Do you mind if I go out for some fresh air?" I asked.

"Of course, no problem! I'll come with you, keep you company," he said eagerly as he went to put on his shoes.

"Actually, if you don't mind, I think I'd rather go alone, just to collect my bearings."

I saw the look of excitement drop from his face into a look of disappointment as I proceeded to change out of my wedding dress into something a little more comfortable. I didn't have much with me since I only brought the sexiest of outfits to my honeymoon. So, I pulled on a strapless dress, threw my leather jacket over it, and slipped into my heels.

"Alright, I'll be here then. I think I'll order some room service. Lobster for two?" he smiled at me, a look of concern washed over his face.

"Sure," I smiled back, leaving the room. "I'll be back shortly."

The moon shined bright in the dark sky as I stood beneath it, popping a cigarette in between my lips.

Why am I even here? I sighed, thinking to myself.

I decided to go for a walk around the resort, anything to clear my head from the never-ending thoughts. The night was calm and quiet, free of noises other than crickets and birds.

Eventually, I found myself standing in front of the hotel lounge, a bar open 24/7 with over 250 different types of bottles and bright lights. I knew I shouldn't have gone in; Avery was back in the room waiting for me with a lobster dinner and probably some champagne. I knew I should've turned back, but I gave into temptation and went in for one drink, or so I promised myself.

"Can I get a double scotch, please? Neat?" I asked the bartender.

It was nearly midnight, but the lounge was still packed with tourists, locals, and honeymooners alike. The music was deafening, and the lights were blinding, but I hadn't felt so relaxed in months. I popped in another cigarette and sat back against a velvet couch. Life was as good as it could get, and I closed my eyes.

"This seat taken?" My thoughts were soon interrupted by the sound of a man's voice.

I slowly opened my eyes and saw a man standing before me, dressed in a white suit and holding a pipe. He had that mysterious look to him that could make any girl drip and swoon. The sexy rugged beard, a golden hairline, and beautiful big blue eyes that made me instantly drool.

"Um, nope. Help yourself," I answered, straightening both my body and my dress before sitting up.

"So, what's a pretty girl like yourself doing here all alone?" he asked.

"What makes you think I'm alone?" I responded coyly, trying to act cute and innocent.

He played along, and I instantly felt a connection. "Well, I just know that, if you were my girl, I would be protective of you all the time. I wouldn't want some sleazeball, like myself, hittin' on you," he smirked.

We continued flirting with each other over the next hour or so until I felt his hand slowly traveling up my dress. I wanted to stop him. I couldn't hurt Avery like this, especially not on our honeymoon. But I also didn't want to. I liked the attention, the touch of a new man. It was exciting and hot. I slowly pulled off my ring before he had a chance to see it and continued to let him run his hand up and down my thigh.

"Your skin is so soft. I feel like I can touch it forever," he grinned as he leaned in closer and ran his lips across my neck.

***

I didn't realize what had happened or how long I'd been out until I woke up the next morning in a strange bed, the man from last night sleeping next to me. That one drink had turned into eight, and my head was pounding as I reached over to grab my phone. Twenty-five missed calls from Avery.

Fuck. I sprung out of bed, quickly got dressed, and bolted out of the room. Luckily, the man was also staying at our hotel so it wasn't a long walk of shame back to my suite.

"I waited all night for you," Avery said, his eyes looking down at the floor, when I walked in. I tried fixing my hair and dress as best I could so Avery wouldn't suspect anything. "I had the whole night all planned out. Lobsters. Champagne. And a romantic night in bed."

"Avery, I…" I began to speak, not really knowing what I would even say.

"Where the hell were you? I thought you were just going out for a walk. You said you'd be back for dinner. Your lobster's sitting in the corner, ready to jump back in the ocean. I didn't even get to enjoy it. I was sick and worried all night."

"Avery, I'm so sorry. I went to the lounge and must've had too much to drink. The bartender told me I fell asleep on one of their couches last night. I'm so, so sorry." Technically, I didn't lie. I did have a couple drinks at the lounge and fell asleep. I just left out the middle man. I wanted to confess. I really did, but he was already so hurt that I couldn't stand hurting him even more.

"That's it? You fell asleep? That's all that happened?" he questioned; his words were suspicious, but his eyes were full of compassion and concern.

"Of course, Avery. You know I would *never* do anything to hurt you. I love you," I said while pulling him into an embrace, slipping my ring back on behind him. "Let me make it up to you. Steak for lunch, on me. The bartender told me about this *amazing* surf and turf place just a mile down the road. Then, we'll pick up a bottle of champagne on the way back and spend the rest of the day in our private hot tub…naked. What do you say?"

"You really know your way to my heart, Xing. Alright, let's do it!" he cheered and gave me a kiss. I was safe, in the clear. Never did I think the consequences of that night would come back to bite me in the ass.

Chapter Sixteen

Avery's Story
The Unexpected Betrayal

"Aria? Are you okay? What happened?" I asked a month later when I found Aria vomiting in the bathroom.

The wedding ceremony and honeymoon were both amazing, and I loved every moment of being married to Aria. I still found it difficult to believe that she was finally mine, for good. All those years of chasing after her and fighting for her love finally paid off. No longer will another man come between us. I could finally relax.

Aria continued to vomit and pointed to a stick sitting on the sink. It was a pregnancy test. Could it really be? I picked it up and saw two stripes. She was pregnant. We were pregnant.

"Oh my god, no way. Is this real?" I asked, still in disbelief.

"Yeah, I'm pregnant. I went out and bought it this morning when I found out I was late," Aria responded, wiping her mouth with a towel.

"Oh my god!" I squealed again. "This is so exciting! I have to tell someone, everyone. I don't even know where to start."

I ran out of the bathroom and called my mom as Aria jumped in the shower to clean herself. "Mom? It's me! Avery! Guess what? You're going to have a grandkid!" I shouted into the phone.

"Huh? What? Why are you calling so early, honey? It's 5am," Mom said, still half asleep, on the other line.

"Aria and I are having a kid. You're going to be a grandma!" I repeated, unable to contain my excitement. "Aren't you happy for us?"

"Avery, honey, you already have kids, Loria and Cooper with what's her face. I'll call you back later," Mom reminded me before hanging up.

Fuck. I completely forgot about my two kids with Liana. I hadn't even thought about them since I called our marriage off the other day on the phone. It was as if my life in New York never happened. I had been so hung up on Aria that I'd forgotten about my responsibilities back home.

The last time I heard from Liana, she texted me saying she was taking the kids to her parents and to expect divorce papers coming my way. However, I had been so distracted with Aria that I didn't even bother texting back, treating my family like I don't even want them.

But I couldn't think about any of that now. I couldn't let the woes back home ruin the life I had now. Aria and I were going to start a family. It's what I'd always wanted since I first laid eyes on her. I had been looking for excuses anyway to stay in LA for as long as I could. I constantly feared flying home to New York and being separated from Aria. And now was the perfect chance. It was a chance for us to start over, to be that perfect family.

***

Over the next several days, I sold my condo in Manhattan and gave up my share of the company to my business partner. Now that a kid was on its way, I didn't have time to run a business anymore. I knew I was taking a huge loss by doing so, but I didn't care. I didn't care about any of it.

***

Several months later, Jesper invited me for a guy's night out at a local bar. He needed to get away from the madhouse he had back home and thought I could use a break also. And boy, did I? Ever since I found out about the baby, I quickly moved Aria and I into a townhome in the suburbs of Los Angeles with the money I had gotten from selling my condo. It cost nearly all I had, but I knew it was going to be worth it. There was no way we could start a family in the tiny apartment Aria was living in.

I spent the rest of what I had saved up on baby-proofing the home and buying all the best supplies I could find, from a luxury stroller to a designer crib, and everything in between. Everything had to be just perfect.

"So, do you guys know what the gender is yet?" Jesper asked me while taking a sip of his beer.

"A boy. We found out just last week. I'm actually really, really excited. I know this sounds bad, but I'm even more excited than when Loria and Cooper were born. Am I a terrible person?" I asked.

"Nah," he replied, taking another sip. "I get it. Aria's the woman of your dreams, has been for decades. Where'd you meet Liana again? At a strip club? That's nowhere near as special as starting a family with your childhood crush. If Rosalie and I didn't end up together, I think I would've always thought about how my life would've been different with her instead."

"How are you guys anyway?" I asked, turning the topic away from me.

"Oh, man, look, I'm really happy for you and Aria and all, but man, raising a kid is rough. I thought I knew Rosalie and all the craziness that came in that little package, but damn, when she's stressed, it's like a whole new monster comes out of her. And trust me, I love my little Angelica, but when she draws on the walls with sharpie and smears mud all over my new furnished kitchen, sometimes I just want to put her in a cage and lock her up. I don't even remember the last time Rosalie and I had sex."

"Ouch, now I see why you needed to come out tonight. I think Aria and I will be fine though. She's great with kids. Did I ever tell you about the time she patched me up when I fell off my bike? Besides, I have some experience raising kids, so I think we'll be alright," I tried to reassure myself.

"Best of luck to you," Jesper said as he raised a toast. "To dads, may we all survive the first year."

I laughed. Jesper was always the humorous one in the group. "Hey, dude, I've been meaning to ask. Do you know if your company's hiring? I sold my business back in Manhattan, and I'm looking for a job in LA, or around the area, at least. With Aria out of work for the next few months, I need to find something quick that will allow me to support us."

"We're always hiring. The turnover rate is like 98%. It's not the best place in the world to work at, but it gets the job done, and the pay is pretty decent. Feel free to put in an application. I'll give you a good word. I do have to warn you though, Xander's working there also. Remember Xander Lee?"

I froze. I remember Xander very well, always ingrained in my brain as the guy who stole Aria from me. I hated him then, and I hated him now. I never wanted to see his stupid face again after what he did. But I didn't really have a choice. The baby was on the way, and I was desperate to find a job. I didn't have the time to submit resumes and set up interviews.

"Oh, yeah, Xander. I remember him. What's he been up to? Family? Kids?" I tried to calm myself down before asking.

"Nothing much, you know he's never really one to settle down. He lived a nomadic life after high school, traveling the world during the past several years, taking up odd jobs here and there to pay for his flights. He hit me up about eight months ago asking if I could get him a job. I guess he ran out of money and needed something a little more stable first before going back out there. Man, sometimes I wish I had the balls to do something like that, just leave everything behind and explore the vast world beyond me. Guess it's a little too late for that now."

"Yeah, I guess." I tried to sympathize with Jesper, but I couldn't relate.

I didn't have a desire to see the world or be a free man. It was just something I never found interest in. Ever since I was a young boy, I would see my parents so happy together while running the house, their restaurant, and taking care of me. It was something I always admired and wanted to experience for myself. I was already living my dream.

***

A few hours later, I went home to my pregnant wife, excited to see her face, and gave her a kiss.

"Hey, honey, did you have fun with Jesper?" Aria asked from the kitchen when I walked in through the door.

I could smell the delicious aroma of roasted garlic and fresh onions as the scent filled the home.

"Oh, it was great! Nice catching up with him, but all I wanted was to come home to you," I grinned as I wrapped my arms around her waist.

"Here, give me your hand," Aria smiled as she guided my hand to the right side of her belly. "Do you feel that?"

"No, what am I supposed to… Wait! Is that a kick? Is the baby kicking?" I asked excitedly.

"Yup, that's him. That's our little boy," she whispered.

"Our little boy, I like the sound of that," I whispered back. "Also, you shouldn't be on your feet. Here, let me finish up dinner, and you go pop your feet up. I didn't buy you that footstool just so you could look at it," I joked.

"But I really think I should finish up. Everything's already started, and you don't know where everything is, and…"

"Aria, Aria, relax! I got this. My dad's a chef, remember? I've worked in the kitchen for years." I looked back to check that nothing was burning on the stove before leading my darling pregnant wife into the living room. "Here you go, nice and comfy," I said as I fluffed several pillows and draped a throw blanket over her shoulders. "Just leave everything to me."

I walked back into the kitchen and saw more pots and pans than I remembered. Aria was always a better cook than me, but damn! How the hell did she have things cooking in four separate locations, all with different sauces and garnishes? She loved cooking and always had a habit of cooking way more than the two of us could eat.

That Aria, our kid is going to be so well fed, I smiled.

"Shit," I muttered as I knocked a pot of boiling water onto the floor. "Jesus!"

"You okay in there?" Aria shouted over to me. Clearly, she could tell I was making a mess.

"Yeah, I'm fine!" I shouted back. "Hey, guess what? I'm applying for a job at Jesper's company. If everything goes smoothly, I should be able to start as early as Thursday. We can finally get that pump you had your eyes on for the past several weeks."

"Jesper's company? Doesn't he work at that dog food factory?" she asked.

"No, not dog food. They turn recycled waste into delicious organic snacks."

"So, dog food," she repeated.

I opened my mouth to say something in defense of the company, but I got nothing. She was right. They were literally making food only dogs would eat. Only in LA could someone get away with something like that.

"I hear Xander's working there," I shouted instead. "Remember him?"

I was hesitant to tell her at first. I was nervous that the name itself would set her hormones into overdrive, and she'd immediately leave me for him. But, then again, she was married to me. To *me*! She vowed to be loyal to me forever no matter what, till death do us part, so I reassured myself that I had nothing to worry about.

"Really? That's exciting. Gosh, I haven't seen or heard from him in ages. I wonder what he's been up to?" Aria's eyes perked up as I mentioned Xander's name.

"Jesper said he's been traveling the world; I don't really know much else."

"Well, if you do end up working there, tell him I say hi." Aria smiled before tucking herself in between several couch pillows.

***

It didn't take long for me to receive an offer after I submitted my resume. My business background was impeccable, and I was a fucking entrepreneur on Wall Street, for god's sake. Companies would be insane to turn me down.

***

"Avery! What's up, man? Long time no see!"

I turned around to the voice screaming my name when I entered the building on my first day of work. The smell was awful, the rooms were stuffy, and I was starting to see why Jesper hated his life so much. I missed my job and life in Manhattan, the posh life, hanging out with celebrities in the most exclusive bars and lounges. But Aria was my life now. If she wanted to stay in LA, then we're staying in LA, no matter how much I hated it.

"Sup, Xander," I responded as I gave Xander a fist bump.

I still hated his guts, but over the years, the hatred had died down. He looked a lot different than I remembered. That scruffy beard was not doing him any justice, and it looked like he hadn't bought new clothes since high school.

"So, what've you been up to man? Jesper told me you recently got married," he asked.

"Yeah, to Aria…"

"Aria? No way!" Xander interrupted me mid-sentence. "Man, I remember Aria. She was always the cutest one in the bunch. But never did I think she'd ever settle down."

"What do you mean?" I asked.

"Well, I'm sure you've heard rumors about why we broke up," he continued.

"Yeah, it's because you wouldn't stop cheating on her." I was getting really angry now. Xander's taunts were getting under my skin.

"Is that what she told you? Man, she was always good at making shit up. No, I never did anything to her. She was the one who cheated. Remember Loe? The exchange student from Vietnam who transferred to our school Sophomore year? It took me a while to realize they weren't just friends. Study groups, my ass. She played me for a fool until I finally caught her fucking him a year later in her car."

I grabbed Xander by the collar of his shirt. "Don't you dare fucking talk about Aria like that! She's the sweetest person I know, and she would *never* cheat on anyone, not even some asshole like you."

"Hey, guys, break it up! Be professional. You two can beat each other up in the parking lot later like everyone else does," Jesper intervened.

"If you don't believe me, ask her yourself," Xander finished before walking away. Definitely a terrible first impression at my new job.

When I finally got home later that night, it was late, and Aria was already in bed. I quietly took off my shoes, changed out of my stinky clothes, and climbed into bed, stroking her arm with my fingers.

"Hmm…hey, how was your first day?" Aria asked, still half asleep.

"It was…fine, I guess. Can I ask you something?" I blurted out. It was late, but I knew that if I didn't ask in that moment, I would never find the courage to.

"Sure, what is it?" she answered.

"Did you ever cheat on Xander?"

"What? What are you talking about?" she asked defensively.

"I was talking to Xander today, and he said he saw you having sex with some guy named Loe during high school."

"That's ridiculous." Aria threw the covers off her and stormed into the bathroom.

However, I still wanted answers and followed her in. "Well, did you?"

"Are you really going to believe some asshole over your own wife?"

"Well, you're not exactly denying it. Why can't you just tell me the truth?" I screamed even louder as the stress began to overwhelm me. When Aria refused to answer back, I got angrier. "You did. You did cheat on him, didn't you? Aria, answer me!" I placed a hand on her shoulder to turn her around. However, when she did, tears began to flow from her eyes as she looked down at the floor. It was wet.

"I think my water broke," she whispered.

In a panic, I ran into the bedroom to gather some things. Despite how much I didn't want to let the topic go, this was *not* the time to stress her out even more. I quickly shoved some blankets and pillows into the back seat of my car before running back up to carry my wife down. Our baby was coming. This was supposed to be the happiest day of my life.

I sped down the freeway, running several stop signs and lights, but I didn't care. The cops in LA had too many criminals to catch to care anyway.

"I need a doctor! My wife is in labor!" I shouted to several paramedics who were standing in front of the emergency room.

As they wheeled her down the halls and into a room, I followed suit, promising her I'd be by her side no matter what. As the doctor told her to push, I held her hand for dear life even as she cracked several of my bones.

"Come on, you can do it, Aria. Just one more push," our doctor said as Aria screamed at the top of her lungs. "Congratulations! It's a boy! Does daddy want to cut the umbilical cord?" she asked as the nurse wrapped a blanket around the baby.

Our baby. My baby. I was so excited and happy that I gave Aria a passionate kiss on the lips and whispered, "You did great, hon," before skipping over.

But when I got to the station, my heart stopped.

"No, this can't be," I whispered to myself.

The baby had blond hair, large blue eyes, and pale skin. Given how Aria and I are both Asian with dark hair and small eyes, there's no way this baby was mine.

"Aria…" I began as I turned back to her, just to find her in tears and regret.

"I'm sorry. I'm so sorry, Avery. It was a mistake! I didn't mean to. I meant to tell you, but I didn't want to hurt you anymore than I already had."

"And how the *hell* do you think I feel now?" my voice raised, and I knocked the vase of flowers beside her bed onto the ground, shattering.

"We'll give you two a moment while we take him to the nursery," the nurse said as they all rushed out of the room, leaving me alone with Aria.

"When?" I demanded.

"Avery, please, let me explain," Aria begged as I closed in on her, my face fuming red.

"I said, when?" I shouted again.

"The night of our honeymoon."

"The night of our… You mean *that's* what you were doing when you didn't come back that night? You told me you ditched our dinner because you passed out at the lounge. But really, you were fucking some guy in his hotel room, weren't you?"

"I'm sorry," she could only whisper as she clearly had no excuses left to give.

"I can't believe this!" I knocked over the other vase and stormed out of the room. "I can't even look at you right now. You disgust me!"

"Avery, please! Come back, come back!" I heard Aria yell on the other side as I closed the door behind me and walked out of the hospital.

That same night, I packed a small bag with my belongings and checked into a motel. I couldn't stand living in a house that had so many of Aria's things in it. I had spent all my savings on these stupid baby things just to find out that he wasn't even mine.

What have I done? I gave up my wife, my kids, my home, my business back in Manhattan, everything, all for a cheater.

I sat at the shitty motel bar and order two shots of whiskey while contemplating the life I was left with. I had it all, the dream I always wanted. If only I hadn't been so selfish and wanted Aria too.

I should've known Aria wasn't any good for me. There were so many signs that warned me to not be with her, starting from all those times she rejected me. But I was too blind to see any of it. All I could see was the dumb childhood crush I had on her, brushing everything else aside. I sighed as I looked around the bar. Everyone else there was either snuggling against their partners or down in the dumps like me. It was a very depressing sight.

"Two more." I gestured to the bartender, pulling the peanuts closer to me.

I didn't know what to do anymore, where my life would take me now. The happiest moment of my life had been ruined by the woman I loved most. It's not like I could even get my old life back. My ex and kids hated me, and I was pretty sure my partner sold my company for a profit. I had no money, no savings, no home, and I felt too ashamed to crawl back to my parents. I had been so confident in this marriage that I couldn't shove another failed relationship in their faces.

I couldn't have them knowing that my child, their prized grandchild, with Aria was a degenerate, a fraud. So, this is who I'd become, drinking alone in a dark and dirty bar with nowhere to go and no one to love.

"Hey, buddy, we're closing soon. I don't give a fuck where you go, but you can't stay here."

My thoughts were disturbed by the bartender pointing at the clock. It was five in the morning, and I had been sitting at the bar for the past four hours. Aria was probably still in the hospital, will probably be for the next several days. I didn't even want to look at that blond child.

I didn't want to go back to my room yet either; it was too sad sleeping in a bed alone again after spending so many nights with Aria. I could always hit up a club or bring someone home with me, but that would only bring me more shame. I was never one to have one-night stands anyway. The last time I tried, I ended up marrying her. No, I was too different from Aria. Even after all she had done to me, I wouldn't be able to hurt her.

I continued to wander the streets of LA, passing by the many tents on skid row and the many cars illegally parked. There were couples holding hands on benches and prostitutes loitering the streets for business. I just wanted to scream at everyone and tell them they'd all end up alone in the end.

It was inevitable. People would always only look out for themselves, and they would have no problem shoving you under the bus to get what they wanted.

Finally, I came to a stop by the ocean shore, my final stop. I came into this country by sea, and it's how I would leave it. My parents should've never come here, nothing but disgusting people and depressing opportunities. I should've given my parents one last call, to say my goodbyes, but then that'll just worry them. Besides, I didn't really care anymore. Nothing mattered. All hope was lost. I felt my pocket vibrate. I looked at the receiver and saw Aria's name.

"Fuck her. Fuck them all," I said as I threw the phone into the ocean. "I'm done."

With my final words, I took a large step in, letting the ocean waters surround me and consume my body. I was part of it now.

Chapter Seventeen

Aria's Story

All Alone Once Again

"Mom, Mom, he's gone. He left. He's gone!" I cried into my phone.

I knew I had fucked up, big time. After Avery stormed out, I tried calling him several times, eighteen to be exact, just to reach his voicemail again and again. I began to panic. I brought this onto myself, but how the hell was I going to raise a newborn all alone? I didn't know the first thing about kids! Plus, I was sure he's going to kick me out of the house since he bought it. I feared that I was going to end up a homeless single mom.

"It's okay, honey, just calm down," Mom repeated on the other line. "What happened?"

I sniffled. "Avery's gone. He left. He found out the kid isn't his, and he just left."

"Oh, Aria, honey. Tell me you didn't," Mom began to speak.

"I did. I didn't mean to! It was an accident. I felt really depressed, and I had a little too much to drink, and one thing led to the next, and now, I think he's gone forever!" I cried like I had never cried before, my heart in so much pain. "I didn't want to do it. I really wanted to commit to this marriage. It was supposed to be just one drink and then back to Avery. But when that other guy touched me, my instincts just took the best of me, and I gave in."

Mom didn't sound too surprised. She knew exactly the feeling I was talking about as it had happened before to her. "It's the curse, honey. All the women in our family have it. We just find it too difficult to say no to cheating. It's in our blood to cheat. I warned you about marrying your best friend, the one person you never wanted to hurt, but you thought you knew better. The Xing women will always cheat. It's a harsh reality we must accept."

"Mom, how do I get him back? I don't want to hurt him anymore. I don't want to cheat on him again. I just want him back," I cried into the phone.

"Just be patient, honey. If the stars align, and you're meant to be together, he'll come back. He loves you. He's Avery. He has, and will, always love you," Mom tried to cheer me up before hanging up the phone.

***

I left the hospital two days later with my newborn son. I hadn't heard a single word from Avery since that day, and I was beginning to worry that he really was done with me. Avery had always been by my side, always there to support me, even when I constantly rejected him. So why was he so distant now? Why was he ignoring all my calls?

When I got home, my heart stopped. All his treasured belongings and half his closet were gone. Maybe he went to stay with Jesper for a few days to cool down. That must be it. I went into the nursery to set the baby down. I couldn't even name him. That was something Avery and I always discussed doing together after we saw the baby.

To do so without him, would be a sin. I couldn't do that to him, even if this baby wasn't his. I just knew that if I explained myself, he'd want to come back and be in this baby's life, to raise him together, just like we'd always planned.

"Hey, Rosalie, it's Aria. Is Avery there?" I asked when Rosalie answered the phone.

"I don't think so… Hey, Jesper!" Rosalie shouted off the receiver. "Have you seen Avery?"

"Nope!" Jesper shouted back. "I haven't heard from him since he took Aria to the hospital. I tried calling him several times to see how the baby was doing, but no answer. If you do get a hold of him though, tell him he's fired if he doesn't show up to work on Monday."

"Sorry, Aria, we have no idea where he is," Rosalie apologized.

"Alright, thanks anyway. Let me know if he turns up," I said before ending the call.

Desperate, I decided to call Xander. I hadn't spoken to him since the breakup, but luckily, his number was still the same. Xander was more than happy to hear my voice. He hadn't heard from Avery either but was excited that I called and invited me over for lunch to catch up. I needed a distraction and some time away from the headaches of the baby, so I dropped him off at Rosalie's and met up with Xander at his apartment.

"Aria, Aria, Aria. So, we finally meet again," Xander grinned when he greeted me at the door, giving me a long and overdue hug.

"Hey, Xander, good seeing you again," I said back.

I felt a feeling of comfort when we hugged. Xander was my first boyfriend, the first boy I ever felt a connection with. All the memories of pain I felt towards him had suddenly disappeared.

He led me over to the living room. There were little to no décor or furniture in the room, like he was obviously renting it temporarily. There was one travel guide on a small wooden table that looked like it was from someone's dumpster, and two folding chairs, one extra for company.

"Nice…place," I said quietly, picking up a picture frame of him and a girl who looked like him. "Who's this?"

"Oh, that's my sister, Ginny," he answered hesitantly.

"I didn't know you have a sister."

"I did," he replied. "She died during senior year of high school."

"I'm so sorry. What happened?" I asked, my eyes sympathetic.

"Her plane crashed on the way to Argentina. She always wanted to travel, see the world. She spent her entire life saving up for that trip, working double shifts and taking up odd jobs wherever she could, giving up her social life. I still remember that day clearly. She had all her bags packed and was psyched to embark on a solo trip to South America. Two days later, my parents got a call that one of the planes malfunctioned and claimed Ginny's life, among others."

"Is that why you travel now? In honor of your sister?"

"Yeah," he sniffled. "Ever since her death, I vowed to live her life for her, carrying out what she always wanted to do. I gave up college and decided to pack my bags instead. I booked a one-way flight to Chile and didn't look back for years. I don't own much. I sold all my possessions because I didn't want to be tied down by materialism. But no matter what, I always carry this picture around. It's the last reminder I have of my sister. She comes with me wherever I go."

"Wow, that's really touching. I never knew that about you. You never really opened up to me when we were younger. I didn't even know you had a soft side," I said gently, careful to avoid saying anything that would trigger him.

"I wanted to impress you. I was scared to show you my vulnerable side because I was afraid you'd take advantage of me and hurt me. I guess I've grown since then. Showing my sensitive side doesn't bother me as much anymore."

I smiled. I never saw Xander in this light before. He was…such an angel, so caring for his sister. I mean, dedicating his entire life in honor of her? I didn't know if I could ever do something like that, even for someone I love.

"I'm thinking Chinese. What do you think?" Xander asked, interrupting my thoughts.

"Huh? Oh, sure, I could go for some Shrimp Lo Mein. I don't remember the last time I had it."

When our food arrived thirty minutes later, Xander pulled out a blanket and a couple pillows, and we laid our feast out on the carpet. I had to admit, it was nice being around Xander again. It reminded me of our dates, when we'd get takeout somewhere, find a park, and just lie on the grass and eat. I missed those days.

"I heard you married Avery," he finally spoke after several minutes of silence. "How's that going?"

I sighed. "Not great. He left a few days ago, and I haven't heard from him since. He's not picking up my calls or anything."

"That sucks. What happened? I mean, Avery isn't the most tempered person in the world, but I know he worships you like a queen, even when we were together. Doesn't seem like him to just leave."

"I don't really want to talk about it," I whispered into my carton of noodles. "Are you dating anyone?"

"No one special, just a couple hookups here and there during my travels. Gotta keep loneliness from setting in somehow."

Xander could tell I was trying to deflect from myself. It didn't take long for him to catch on and move away from the topic of Avery. "I have an idea! Let's play Truth or Dare. Remember how we used to play all the time as kids?"

I smiled, "Sure. I'll go first. Truth or Dare?"

"Dare."

"I dare you to hop on one leg while chugging some vodka."

"Is that it? Easy! I used to do that all the time." I watched as Xander grabbed a bottle from his fridge and started hopping. He was so confident at first…until the liquor entered between his lips, and he started choking, spilling vodka all over the carpet before falling soon after. He started laughing hysterically as he collided with the ground, his tongue licking the fibers like they were mini lollipops.

"Hmmm, nothing more delicious than a freshly-soaked carpet," he laughed. "Alright, Ms., or should I say Mrs., Aria Xing. Truth or Dare?"

"Truth," I said confidently, hoping for an easy one.

"Do you still have feelings for me?" he asked.

Shit, what did I get myself into? "I…uh…" I guessed, in hindsight, I *was* feeling something towards Xander. Not having Avery in my life, that spark in my life, that hand to hold whenever I needed it, was beginning to make me feel extremely lonely. I hated the way Xander treated me in the past, all the times he stared at other women while we were together, but I couldn't help but let all that go now. I was beginning to see Xander in a different light.

"Just kidding!" he shouted as I was deep in thought. "I really had you going there, didn't I?" he smirked.

"You ass!" I laughed, throwing my wooden chopsticks at him. "I don't wanna play anymore."

"Aw, come on, Aria. You always were a sore loser."

"You're the loser!" I became defensive and lunged at him, tackling him to the ground. "Take it back! Take it back!" I yelled as I wrestled his arms to the ground.

However, Xander was much stronger than me and resisted my hold. Instead, he grabbed me by my arms and flipped me over so my back was against the ground, piercing my arms into the carpet.

"Oh, sweet, innocent, Aria. You were never a match for me," Xander winked as he stared at me, refusing to take his eyes off me. "Wow, I never realized how long your eyelashes are."

I fell silent. The way Xander looked at me sent shivers through my body, like I was possessed and couldn't look away. "Xander…" I whispered.

Suddenly, without saying a word, Xander slowly leaned down to kiss me, his chapped lips caressing mine, my arms still pierced to the ground. I knew I should've pulled away, but I couldn't. I wanted him as much as he wanted me. He lowered his body closer to mine, pressing his hip into my waist and kissed me even harder. Taking it as a sign, he began to undress me, pulling my shirt over my head and kissing my bare stomach.

"No, I can't!" I shouted abruptly, pushing him away.

"Why? What's wrong?" he asked.

"I…I can't do this. I'm in love with Avery," I stuttered, grabbing my shirt and running out the door.

***

Over the next several months, I waited and waited for Avery to come back, to return my calls, to be there in my and my son's life. He still remained nameless; almost six months old, and still without a name. I wouldn't be able to live with myself if I had gone ahead and named him. My son was the only thing still tying me to Avery, even if he wanted nothing to do with either of us.

***

Years went by, decades went by, and I never heard from Avery again. Perhaps he'd moved on, found a new wife, and settled down with his new family. Perhaps he went back to his old family. But still, I remained hopeful,

hopeful that our love was strong enough that he'll come find me one day, and we can be together again.

My parents raised my son until they passed away. Ary, they called him, a combination of Aria and Avery. Soon, he grew up and moved out to start his own family, leaving me alone once again.

One dark night, at the old age of 92, my heart started to give out on me. I was rushed to the hospital but failed to make it there alive.

"I love you, Avery," I whispered to myself, my last words ever said.

Avery & Aria
The Story of Star-Crossed Lovers

Avery & Aria

Avery & Aria
The Story of Star-Crossed Lovers

Avery & Aria

Avery & Aria